Elizabeth had already filled seven pages of a yellow legal pad with her ideas and observations about the thefts. "Both items belonged to the di Riminis . . . one missing from the train . . . one from the château . . . ," she read. "The diamond necklace was stolen from Antonia's room in the château—and the di Riminis' family heirloom was stolen from the countess's luggage."

Elizabeth circled the word *heirloom* and drew a big question mark next to it. She didn't know what the heirloom object was exactly and made a mental note to find out.

Elizabeth realized that she and Jessica were the most obvious suspects. They were the only people who had been on the train *and* who were staying at the château.

Except for the countess and Antonia, of course, Elizabeth reflected. The more she considered the possibilities, the more convinced she was of the countess's guilt. All her bluster and rage in the servants' wing that morning might have been nothing more than an attempt to divert suspicion from herself.

Suddenly the door burst open and Jessica rushed in. "Come on, Liz, let's go!"

Elizabeth jumped up, responding to the urgency in her twin's voice. "Go where?" she asked, following Jessica to the stairs.

"To find the jewel," Jessica hissed.

Elizabeth's mouth snapped shut, and she shivered with excitement. *We just might crack this case,* she thought.

Visit the Official Sweet Valley Web Site on the Internet at:

http://www.sweetvalley.com

TO CATCH
A THIEF

Written by
Kate William

Created by
FRANCINE PASCAL

BANTAM BOOKS
NEW YORK · TORONTO · LONDON · SYDNEY · AUCKLAND

RL 6, age 12 and up

TO CATCH A THIEF
A Bantam Book / August 1997

Sweet Valley High® is a registered trademark of Francine Pascal.
Conceived by Francine Pascal.
Produced by Daniel Weiss Associates, Inc.
33 West 17th Street
New York, NY 10011.
Cover photography by Michael Segal.

All rights reserved.
Copyright © 1997 by Francine Pascal.
Cover art copyright © 1997 by Daniel Weiss Associates, Inc.
No part of this book may be reproduced or transmitted
in any form or by any means, electronic or mechanical,
including photocopying, recording, or by any information
storage and retrieval system, without permission in
writing from the publisher.
For information address: Bantam Books.

ISBN: 0-553-57067-6

Published simultaneously in the United States and Canada

Bantam Books are published by Bantam Books, a division of Bantam
Doubleday Dell Publishing Group, Inc. Its trademark, consisting of the
words "Bantam Books" and the portrayal of a rooster, is Registered in U.S.
Patent and Trademark Office and in other countries. Marca Registrada.
Bantam Books, 1540 Broadway, New York, New York 10036.

PRINTED IN THE UNITED STATES OF AMERICA

OPM   0 9 8 7 6 5 4 3 2 1

To Jordan Silverman

Chapter 1

Elizabeth Wakefield felt as if she'd drifted into a fairy tale. *Where else would I be riding on horseback in the moonlight alongside a handsome prince?* she wondered. The cool night air was scented by salty breezes blowing off the Mediterranean Sea, with a whiff of the lavender that grew abundantly all over the island.

Can all this really be happening? Elizabeth asked herself. She glanced at Prince Laurent de Sainte-Marie, riding beside her on his white stallion. Tall and lean, with broad shoulders and sharp features, Laurent was incredibly handsome—the very image of a regal hero. He was the oldest son of a royal European family and the heir to the de Sainte-Marie fortune. He was also a wonderful person, warm and down-to-earth.

Elizabeth and her twin sister, Jessica, were working as au pair girls for the summer, taking care of Laurent's three young siblings. The job had been Jessica's idea. She'd jumped at the chance to spend her vacation on a private island off the coast of southern France. But the de Sainte-Maries had wanted an older girl with more experience. They'd agreed to hire Jessica only if they could also find a second girl to share the job. Immediately she'd starting working on Elizabeth, trying to convince her to take the second au pair position.

Elizabeth had balked at her twin's plan. The idea of spending the entire summer so far away from her home in Sweet Valley, California, hadn't appealed to her at all. But Jessica had worn her down—as usual.

She had regretted caving in to Jessica when she'd had to say good-bye to her longtime boyfriend, Todd Wilkins. The thought of having to spend months away from him had hurt deeply. But apparently Todd hadn't felt the same way.

Elizabeth felt a pang of regret as she recalled their last time together, the evening before she'd left for France. Todd had broken up with her, claiming that long-distance relationships were too difficult to maintain. She'd felt terribly wounded and had thought the pain would never end.

She certainly hadn't planned to get involved

2

with anyone else for some time. But then a handsome prince had come into her life. . . .

"Here we are," Laurent said, slowing his horse to a trot as they came over a hill.

Elizabeth brought her black mare to a stop, shifting her weight as the horse sidestepped a few paces. "I can't get over how beautiful this place is," she murmured as she gazed down at the Château d'Amour Inconnu, the summer home of the de Sainte-Marie family. The château looked like a fairy-tale castle, its white stone walls glimmering in the moonlight. Several spiked gables jutted up from the roof around the main tower, which was covered with red stone shingles.

Laurent helped Elizabeth down from the mare. "I think Cendrillon likes you," he said. He pronounced his words with a melodic French accent that Elizabeth thought was delightful.

Elizabeth stroked the animal's glossy black fur. "I like her too," she replied.

She watched as Laurent looped the horses' reins around a tree trunk.

"Cendrillon means Cinderella, doesn't it?" Elizabeth asked as she and Laurent hiked down the hill, hand in hand.

Laurent nodded. "The mare's name used to be Noir because her color is like the night," he told her. "But the first time we were outfitting her for the horseshoes, she pulled the cross-tie out of the wall and escaped with only three of the shoes attached to her hooves. After that everyone called her Cendrillon."

Elizabeth laughed. "How disappointing," she said wryly. "I was expecting a much more romantic explanation."

Laurent chuckled. "The blacksmith was also disappointed."

As they drew closer to the château Elizabeth noticed that the de Sainte-Maries' dinner party was still going on, even though it was after midnight. The French doors to the formal parlor were open, and several guests were congregated on the stone veranda. The soft strains of a flute and piano duet seemed to float on the breeze.

Elizabeth grimaced as she caught sight of the countess di Rimini and her daughter, Antonia, who were vacationing with the de Sainte-Maries for the summer. They had traveled to the château on the same train as the twins and were two of the biggest snobs Elizabeth had ever met. On the train the countess had created a big scene about having to ride in the second-class car. Then she had created an even bigger scene by accusing everyone in the train of having stolen a precious heirloom from her suitcase.

"I think we should avoid the main entrances," Laurent suggested.

Elizabeth nodded. Laurent had skipped the party to be with her, and she understood why he might want to avoid being seen. "Are you going to be in big trouble with your parents?" she asked.

4

Laurent gently pulled her into his arms. "No matter the cost, I wouldn't have missed this time with you," he said.

Elizabeth smiled up at him. In the moonlight his dark blue eyes shimmered with emotion. "I'm glad," she replied. "But—"

He lowered his lips to hers, pushing her words right out of her mind with a deep, searing kiss. Elizabeth wrapped her arms around his neck and held on tightly, as if she might melt into the ground without his support.

"Oh, Laurent," she murmured. "This is all so . . ." She breathed deeply and rested her forehead against his chest. "I can't even describe how I feel right now."

"Neither can I," he whispered.

A sudden burst of laughter on the veranda broke the spell. Elizabeth sighed in disappointment. "I can go the rest of the way by myself," she offered. Laurent was staying in a small private cottage on the north side of the island, some distance from the château.

He squeezed her hand. "What kind of a prince would I be if I didn't see my lovely damsel safely to her door?" he chided her jokingly. "But don't worry. I have an idea."

He steered Elizabeth away from the château. "Have you discovered the secret tunnels yet?"

Elizabeth raised her eyebrows. "Secret tunnels?"

"But of course," he replied with a laugh. "They are a standard feature in old European castles."

"Sounds interesting," Elizabeth said. "Lead the way. The last thing I feel like tonight is another run-in with the di Rimini duo. Sometimes I get the impression that they don't consider Jessica and me worthy of breathing the same air. We are such *lowly* servants, after all," she added sarcastically.

Laurent cleared his throat and chuckled nervously without comment. Elizabeth narrowed her eyes, wondering about his strange reaction. *Maybe he feels embarrassed about his family's friendship with such horrid snobs,* she thought. She decided to drop the subject. The di Riminis were nothing to her and Laurent, especially on such a glorious evening.

"Where are we going?" Elizabeth asked as they crept into a small, enclosed garden. Its high stone walls were covered with dark climbing vines. Just inside the iron gate a pair of stone lions flanked the entrance. A grassy path curved into a shadowy jungle of flowering bushes.

"Trust me," Laurent said reassuringly.

Elizabeth felt giddy with a sense of adventure as Laurent led her farther into the garden. The air was perfumed with honeysuckle and rose, and the wind whispered through the tangled dark foliage.

They came to a white stone shed that seemed to glow like a ghost in the moonlit night. Laurent reached for the latch on the wrought iron door and pushed it open. It swung inward with an ominous-sounding creak.

Elizabeth gulped. "We have to go in *there?*" she asked nervously as she peered into the black interior.

Laurent rubbed the back of her neck. "It's perfectly safe," he assured her. "I've been sneaking through these tunnels since I was a child."

"I'm glad I wasn't *your* au pair," Elizabeth muttered dryly. Steeling her courage, she followed him through the doorway.

Elizabeth was immediately engulfed in blackness. She felt her way along a cold, damp wall, skimming her fingers over the bumpy ridges in the stones. With her sight disabled, her remaining senses grew sharper. The echo of their voices and footsteps into the distance told her they were in a cavernous tunnel of some sort. She sniffed the air and noticed it smelled like wet dirt and chalk.

"These tunnels were built in the twelfth century," Laurent explained. "They were used by the royal family to escape the invasions of their enemies. In the time of the French Revolution noble families hid down here from the mobs, and during World War II the Jews found refuge from the Nazis."

"Wow!" Elizabeth exclaimed. "There's so much history in here. I wish these walls could tell us everything."

"I'm sure there is more than anyone knows,"

Laurent said. "Imagine all the *rendezvous en secret*—secret meetings—that have taken place over the years." He chuckled. "These walls could tell better stories than the American soap operas."

Elizabeth laughed. "As long as they don't tell on *us*." She flinched as her fingers slipped across a patch of slime on the wall.

The tunnel gradually widened enough for her and Laurent to walk side by side. "How did the Château d'Amour Inconnu get its name?" Elizabeth asked. "It means unfamiliar or unknown love, doesn't it?"

"Yes," Laurent replied. "There is a legend of sorts."

"Well—," Elizabeth prompted, gently squeezing his hand. "I hope it's more exciting than the one about how Cendrillon got *her* name," she added jokingly.

Laurent said nothing for several seconds. "Long ago a prince fell in love with a young maiden," he began at last. "But their love was doomed. And things for them ended badly."

"What happened?" Elizabeth asked, intrigued.

Laurent cleared his throat. "The prince married another; the maiden turned into a bird."

"That's it?" Elizabeth protested, laughing.

"It's a worn-out story and not so interesting to me. I prefer modern times." He lifted their entwined hands to his lips and placed a soft kiss on her wrist. "And modern love stories."

Chuckling, Elizabeth made a mental note to ask

about the legend at the château. One of the servants could probably fill her in on the missing details.

The passageway narrowed again. "We're almost at the end," Laurent told her.

Elizabeth sensed the floor rising at a steep incline, forcing her leg muscles to work much harder. She also noticed faint, luminescent patterns on the walls. "I can actually see something," she said.

"There are open panels near the ceiling in this part, which allow in the moonlight," Laurent explained.

He reached for her hand and guided her around a corner. "Here we are," he said.

Straining her eyes, Elizabeth noticed the faint outline of a small door several feet from the ground.

"That's strange," he suddenly murmured. "It's not locked. This entrance is usually kept bolted shut. Someone must have used it recently."

As Laurent opened the door a wedge of light filtered into the darkness. Elizabeth breathed a sigh of relief.

Laurent glanced at her over his shoulder, his eyebrows raised. "You doubted me?" he teased.

"Not for a minute!" she countered. "But I'm not cut out to be a mole. I'm from southern California—born in sunlight."

He laughed at that, then poked his head through the doorway. "All clear," he whispered.

Bracing his arms on the ledge, Laurent hoisted himself up through the opening, then reached down to help Elizabeth.

She crawled through the doorway and found herself crouched beneath a dusty staircase. She noticed the familiar brown-and-tan tiles that covered the floor. "This is the servants' wing," she whispered. The rooms she and her twin had been assigned were just up the stairs. Elizabeth flashed a broad smile at Laurent. "I'm truly amazed."

"I'm amazed also," he said, his voice low and sexy. "By you, Elizabeth."

She saw the passionate look in his eyes. Her mouth went dry. Laurent moved closer and slowly pulled her into his arms. "This night with you has been so special," he said. "If only . . ."

Holding her breath, Elizabeth waited for him to continue. Instead he lowered his lips to hers for a deep, powerful kiss that seemed to go on and on. Elizabeth felt as if their hearts were beating together, as if their souls were entwined. *I'm really and truly in love,* she thought. *With a prince!*

In her small room in the servants' wing of the Château d'Amour Inconnu, Jessica Wakefield snuggled closer to Jacques Landeau. Although they'd been apart for nearly a week, it seemed she'd been waiting for him forever.

Jacques shifted slightly, squeaking the rusty springs of her narrow bed. "I have missed you so, *mon ange,*" he whispered into her ear, his sexy French accent melting her heart.

Jessica had known that coming to France for

the summer would turn out to be a fabulous, romantic adventure. But falling in love with Jacques was even more wonderful than she'd imagined. Not only was he gorgeous, with warm brown eyes and curly dark hair, but he also happened to be from a royal family. His father, Louis Landeau, was the duke of Norveaux.

Jessica had met Jacques and his father a week earlier, at the train station in Paris. She had been struggling with her luggage and had begged her twin for help. In response Elizabeth had spouted off a litany of I-told-you-so's in an annoying, bossy-older-sister tone of voice and had marched off without a backward glance. Of course, *Elizabeth* had managed to pack all her things into two bags and had worn sensible shoes.

Jessica's arms, back, and shoulders had been throbbing painfully under the heavy load of her many bags, and her new leather sandals had blistered her feet. Suddenly the hottest guy she'd ever seen and a distinguished-looking gentleman had appeared at her side. After introducing himself and his father, Jacques had offered to carry Jessica's luggage. Then the Landeaus had boarded the same train as the twins. Jacques and Jessica had sat side by side, talking and laughing for hours . . . and somewhere along the way Jessica had fallen totally in love.

Jessica sighed deeply and wrapped her arms

around Jacques's neck. "I missed you too," she said. "This week has been miserable without you."

He gently ran his fingers up and down her arm, setting off a cascade of tingles all through her body. "You and I, Jessica, we share something that is so . . . *magnifique*. With you I feel like I am at home in my heart. You inspire me to many dreams."

Jessica snuggled closer. "What kind of dreams?"

Jacques's brown eyes glimmered. "I dare to see in my mind a future with you," he whispered. "I imagine new things we shall discover together. I wish to show you the many wonderful places I have traveled. You are so full of life . . . all the days with you become a beautiful adventure."

Jessica basked with pleasure. "I like your dreams."

Jacques leaned over her, bracing himself with his elbow. "Two years ago my father and I made a trip to Morocco. We stayed in a white palace that dazzled the eyes in the bright desert sun. And the sounds in the village, the people and the animals, the markets . . . they were like a strange, exotic song."

Jessica closed her eyes, letting his words paint a picture in her mind. She imagined herself draped in silk and jewels, riding with Jacques on a camel across the sandy desert. . . .

"Another time we joined with a safari in central Africa," Jacques continued.

Jessica wrinkled her nose. "Did you have to

sleep in tents and fight off giant killer mosquitoes?"

Jacques grinned sheepishly. "The tents, they were appointed as lavishly as a luxury hotel, with soft beds and elegant furniture. But the mosquitoes, they are pesky like everywhere."

"What about the wild lions and rhinoceroses?" Jessica asked. "Wasn't it dangerous?"

"It was not," Jacques replied. "We don't go too near the wild animals. We shoot them only with the cameras, with the lenses that are, how you say . . . long-range. But of course, my father would advise I tell of my courage in facing a hundred fierce lions, so as to impress you," he added with a laugh.

Jessica grinned, recalling Louis Landeau's blatant matchmaking efforts and indiscreet romantic advice to both her and Jacques during the train ride from Paris. "Your father is too much," she said jokingly.

Jacques rolled his eyes. "*That* he is. When we went to Saint-Tropez last month, he fell in love with three different women in only one day."

Jessica laughed, then put on a mock-fierce expression. "I hope you're not planning to follow his example!"

"Not me." He cupped her jaw in his hand and gazed into her eyes. "My heart is taken," he breathed. "It belongs to you."

Tears of joy pooled in Jessica's eyes. "You're crying?" Jacques said, his voice filled with concern.

Jessica flashed him a watery smile. "I'm happy."

"I am also," he told her. "Happier than ever in my life." He brushed his fingertip over her lips. "I love you, Jessica."

Jacques kissed her then, a deep, passionate kiss that went on and on. A million emotions swirled through Jessica, all of them wonderful. It was as if she and Jacques were sealing an unspoken promise to each other that would last forever.

When the kiss ended, Jacques brushed a lock of hair behind her ear. "I only wish I could stay longer. But I must go."

Jessica frowned. "Why?" she demanded. "You just got here."

Jacques sat up and turned to her. "My father is waiting for me," he replied.

"I'm sure he won't mind if you're a little late," she insisted, reaching for him again.

"Believe me, I'd stay longer if I could," Jacques told her.

Jessica scooted back against the headboard and crossed her arms. It seemed Jacques was already taking her for granted, even though their relationship was barely a week old. "Maybe you're not as excited to see me as you say you are?"

"This is not true," Jacques argued. He pushed his hand through his hair and exhaled sharply. "I wish I could explain. . . . But I really must go."

Jessica felt a quick flare of irritation. She raised her chin and gave Jacques a cold look. "So, go," she said tersely.

Groaning, Jacques pulled her into his arms and hugged her tightly. "Don't be angry with me, please." He leaned back and framed her face with his hands. "You torture my soul, Jessica."

Seeing the anguish in his eyes, Jessica softened. "OK, I won't be angry, but only if you promise to come back tomorrow."

Jacques took her hand and raised it to his lips. "But of course, *mon ange*. Nothing can keep me away."

That's better, Jessica thought, grinning.

Jacques kissed her palm, then held it against his cheek. "I'll be counting the moments until I see you again."

Jessica sighed. She couldn't help being charmed by his romantic words and his irresistible French accent. "I'll be counting the moments too," she whispered.

Huddled under the staircase in Laurent's arms, Elizabeth heard a sound at the top of the stairs. She froze. "I think someone's coming," she whispered. Laurent pulled her farther into the shadows and kissed her again.

Elizabeth laughed softly against his lips. "How are we going to explain ourselves if we get caught?" she murmured.

Laurent sighed and lowered his arms. "You're right,

of course. Maybe I will see you tomorrow?" he asked.

"I'd like that," Elizabeth replied. "I have to take care of the children in the morning, but I'll be free after lunch."

Laurent touched his lips to her forehead in a kiss that was as soft as a feather. "I'd better go and let you get your rest," he said. "You'll need your energy; I know what my little brother and sisters are like when they first wake up."

"I'll be fine," Elizabeth assured him, even though she had her doubts. Taking care of the three young de Sainte-Marie children was quite a challenge, even with a good night's sleep.

Laurent touched the side of her face, then pushed a lock of her hair behind her ear. "*Bonsoir,* Elizabeth."

"Good night," she whispered.

Gingerly picking her steps, she crept up the long, winding staircase to her room. She felt a twinge of guilt as she walked past Jessica's closed door. Elizabeth had shirked her au pair responsibilities that evening, forcing her sister to pick up the slack. *I'll have to make it up to her somehow,* she decided as she entered her own room.

The twins had gotten into a huge fight when they'd first started working at the château. Jessica hadn't taken her duties as an au pair very seriously, and Elizabeth had been furious with her. They hadn't spoken for days and had

16

worked alternating shifts to avoid spending time together.

Although they'd patched up their differences since then, they had agreed to continue working in shifts so that they could each enjoy some time off. Elizabeth was supposed to have worked that evening, but then Prince Laurent had come along on his horse. . . . *Jessica of all people should understand why I ditched her and the children tonight,* Elizabeth thought with a laugh.

Younger by four minutes, Jessica lived her life as if it were one big adventure. She rarely stopped to consider her actions, always jumping blindly into any situation that promised fun and excitement. She had a knack for getting herself into trouble—and more often than not, the trouble had to do with a guy. It was Elizabeth who usually got her out of the mess. Jessica was extremely intelligent, but somehow the idea of learning from her past mistakes seemed to be beyond her comprehension.

Though the twins were identical, with shoulder-length blond hair, blue-green eyes, and lean, athletic figures, the similarities stopped at the surface. The differences in their personalities were as vast as the ocean. Unlike Jessica, Elizabeth planned her actions carefully. She was known as the serious twin, and in most instances the label fit. Her ambition was to become a professional writer someday, and she took pride in the column she wrote for Sweet Valley High's student newspaper, the *Oracle*.

Elizabeth sometimes felt as if she were *Jessica's* baby-sitter, which had caused problems between them when they tried to take care of the de Sainte-Marie children together. But even before they had arrived at the Château d'Amour Inconnu, Elizabeth had sensed that her younger twin was going to get herself into mischief that summer.

Of course, Jessica's attitude that she was coming to France for a "romantic adventure" was a sure sign of trouble. She was hard enough to manage in her usual fun-loving state of mind, but Jessica Wakefield in *love* was an unstoppable force. Even in the train station in Paris she'd attracted a too-smooth guy to sweep her off her feet!

Elizabeth rolled her eyes at the memory of Jacques Landeau and his father, Louis, who was supposed to be a duke. Jessica had been thoroughly enchanted by them, especially Jacques. But there had been something strange about them. They were friendly enough . . . a little *too* friendly, in Elizabeth's opinion. She had breathed a deep sigh of relief when the Landeaus had finally gotten off the train. After all, the twins would probably never see Jacques Landeau again, and even Jessica couldn't get into much trouble on a small, private island.

Elizabeth turned on the lamp on her dresser and removed a neatly folded nightshirt from the top drawer. She liked to have fun as much as her twin did, but to her, fun meant losing herself in a great novel or watching old movies with her best friends in Sweet Valley, Enid Rollins and Maria Slater. *And spending quiet moments alone with Todd,* she added wistfully to herself.

"No!" Elizabeth spat, slamming her drawer shut. "I'm *not* going to think about Todd!"

She kicked off her shoes, then placed them in front of the nonworking fireplace next to the dresser. "Todd is history," she declared, forcing herself not to wince at the sound of the words. *He* had broken up with *her.* It wasn't her fault that their relationship had ended, and she refused to spend another minute wallowing in misery.

Besides, she had Laurent in her life now, a real Prince Charming.

Elizabeth turned off the lamp and plopped down across her narrow, four-poster bed. Moonlight shone through the windows, bathing everything in pale blue light. An image of Laurent's handsome face floated into her mind. *What an awesome, phenomenal, incredible night,* she thought, reliving the way it felt to be in Laurent's arms . . . to kiss him. . . .

During the airplane flight to France a week

earlier, Elizabeth had fallen asleep and dreamed that she was lost in a field of wildflowers during a storm. A young man on a white horse had rescued her, and together they'd galloped away.

At the time Elizabeth had dismissed the dream as ridiculous nonsense. But on her first day as an au pair, she'd gotten lost in the winding topiary maze on the grounds of the de Sainte-Marie estate while chasing after six-year-old Pierre. When she'd finally caught up with him, he was crouched behind a tall bush, watching Laurent practice his fencing in front of his small cottage. Something about him had stirred Elizabeth's memory, but she hadn't been able to figure out why.

The following evening she had gotten lost in the topiary maze again. The sky had suddenly turned dark. Lightning had flashed, and rain had begun to pour. Cold, wet, and shivering, Elizabeth had panicked. Finally she'd found her way to the prince's private cottage—his hideaway from the pressures of royal life.

Laurent had seemed shocked to see her standing there when he'd opened the door. But he'd quickly recovered and had led her inside, where a cozy fire was burning in the hearth.

Elizabeth sighed deeply, remembering how great it had felt to come in from the cold. Curled up in a wool blanket, sipping hot tea, she had spent the entire night talking and laughing with Laurent.

Elizabeth had been surprised to discover how much they had in common despite their very different backgrounds. Laurent was serious-minded, deep, and silly all at the same time. But as much as she'd enjoyed his company, she hadn't expected anything more than a casual friendship.

Elizabeth certainly hadn't expected him to show up at the château that evening with two horses and a picnic basket. Then later Laurent had surprised her even more when he'd told her about a dream *he'd* had, in which a beautiful blond girl had appeared in the middle of a huge ball. In the dream, he had made his way over to the mysterious stranger, but just as he was about to lead her to a dance, she vanished.

"But now the dream has come true," he had said to Elizabeth. Then Elizabeth had suddenly realized why he had seemed familiar to her. Laurent was the guy who had rescued her in her dream.

Thinking about it now, Elizabeth shivered. The logical part of her mind insisted that it must be just a coincidence that she and Laurent had dreamed about each other before they'd met. But her heart felt differently.

Elizabeth snuggled under her blanket and closed her eyes. *Are Laurent and I* destined *to be together?* she wondered.

Chapter 2

Jessica opened her eyes slowly and smiled, her whole body tingling with excitement as she awoke to another beautiful day at the Château d'Amour Inconnu. Sunlight streamed through the open windows. A soft gust of tangy sea air blew into the room, fluttering the sheer lace curtains. On the horizon the Mediterranean shimmered in the early morning light. Even her tiny room seemed less shabby, though the walls were still a ghastly shade of dirty yellow and the chest of drawers and bureau on the other side of the room were still old and rickety. But thanks to Jacques, the world seemed brighter.

Jessica stretched out her arms, yawning, and exhaled with a deep, satisfied sigh. "I *knew* I was going to fall in love this summer," she murmured.

She reached under her pillow and pulled out the red velvet jewelry case she'd put there for safekeeping. Her heart fluttered as she opened the lid and lifted a beautiful emerald pendant by its delicate gold chain. The stone dazzled her eyes.

Jacques had given it to her the day they'd met, just before they'd parted. He'd taken her to a private compartment on the train for a special good-bye. Jessica had gasped when she'd seen the huge stone, but Jacques had admitted that it was a fake. "Someday I'll replace it with the real thing," he'd declared. Then they'd shared their first kiss. . . .

Jessica felt warm tingles dancing up and down her spine at the memory. Meeting Jacques was a dream come true, although she was sure her twin wouldn't agree. For some reason Elizabeth had seemed totally against Jacques from the start. *What a spoilsport!* Jessica thought, giggling.

She raised the pendant, watching the sunlight filter through the beautiful stone. *I don't care if it is a fake; I think it's beautiful!* she decided.

She slipped the jewel into the case and tucked it back under her pillow. "I have a feeling my life is about to get very exciting," she whispered into the empty room.

Before arriving at the Château d'Amour Inconnu a week ago, Jessica had imagined herself living in luxury, attending lavish dinner parties, and hobnobbing with the rich and famous. But she'd quickly realized that *au pair* was just a fancy name for *baby-sitter* and that *working* for royalty didn't mean she'd be *treated* royally.

The de Sainte-Maries weren't harsh or rude, but they didn't go out of their way to make the twins feel comfortable either. Despite the number of elegant, *vacant* suites in the château, she and Elizabeth had been assigned two cramped, ugly rooms in the servants' wing. Jessica had been forced to store most of her clothes in Elizabeth's closet because the one in her own room was too small.

Instead of sitting in the posh dining room and eating from priceless heirloom china, the twins had to eat their meals in the kitchen with the children and servants. They hadn't been invited to socialize with any of the important guests who visited the château either.

But Jessica was sure all that was about to change—thanks to Jacques. When the de Sainte-Maries found out that she was dating a duke's son, they would surely start treating her much better.

Suddenly Jessica heard a soft tapping at the door. Even though it was barely six o'clock in the morning, instinctively she knew it was Jacques. *He really is eager to see me again,* she thought. *How romantic!* Grabbing her short, blue silk robe off the floor, she jumped out of bed.

But before she reached the door, it opened. Jacques gasped, obviously shocked to see Jessica. "I—I did not expect . . . that is, I w-was hoping to . . . surprise you while you slept," he stammered.

Jessica smiled tenderly. "That's so sweet." She moved closer and wrapped her arms around his

24

neck. "I couldn't sleep, thinking about you. . . ."

Jacques swept her off her feet in a passionate embrace and carried her back to her bed. Bracing his hands on either side of her face, he leaned over her and kissed her deeply.

Jessica let herself get caught up in the delightful sensation. But after a few seconds she pushed him away and sat up. She didn't want him to get overly confident about their relationship. She knew how important it was to keep guys hanging and wanting more.

"What's wrong?" he asked.

Jessica tossed back her hair and flashed him a flirty grin. "Nothing. I just need a few minutes by myself," she replied.

When he made no move to get up, Jessica walked to the door and opened it for him. She stared at him expectantly. "See you later, Jacques."

He responded with a smooth, challenging grin. "I'm not ready to go."

Hearing the arrogant tone in his voice, Jessica felt her temper flaring. "This is *my* room, and *I* say you're leaving."

"But I have only just arrived," he pleaded.

"And now you're *leaving*," she repeated.

Jacques exhaled loudly and slowly rose to his feet. He crossed the room and took Jessica into his arms again. "You are a very stubborn girl."

Jessica smiled up at him. "You're very stubborn yourself. And if you don't get out of here in three seconds . . ." She shot him a wide-eyed, threatening look.

He kissed her forehead. "What will you do?" he whispered teasingly.

"Out!" Jessica instructed with a laugh. She placed her hands flat against his chest and shoved him hard, pushing him through the open doorway. Before he could react, she stepped back and slammed the door shut.

"Wait!" he called to her through the door. "I must speak to you about—"

"*Later*, Jacques," Jessica replied. She leaned against the door, waiting until she heard his footsteps walking away.

Now what am I going to wear today? she asked herself. She wanted to look spectacular when she waltzed into Princess de Sainte-Marie's sitting room with Jacques at her side.

My days as a nobody around here are about to end, Jessica thought.

"Pierre, stop playing with your food," Elizabeth scolded, trying to inject a forceful tone into her voice. She and the children were having breakfast in the nursery because the kitchen was being scrubbed and polished. Apparently it was a monthly ritual at the château, overseen by the de Sainte-Maries' head chef himself.

In contrast to the heavy antique furniture in the other rooms of the château, the decor in the nursery was strictly modern. The walls were covered with cartoon wallpaper. The colorful pattern was repeated in the curtains that hung on the wide bay window. Ceiling-high, wooden bookcases stood on either side, one filled entirely with English books. A bright orange play unit with a slide, stairs, tunnel, and pull-up bar stood in one corner of the room. Along the wall blue-and-yellow built-in cubby boxes held building blocks, games, and stuffed animals.

The de Sainte-Marie children were adorable, with dark curly hair and big dark eyes, but they were also incredibly rambunctious and exhausting. They had enthusiastically helped Elizabeth wash and set the table in the nursery.

Now, as they shared the fresh croissants, fruit, and milk the kitchen staff had sent up, Elizabeth tried to maintain order. Six-year-old Pierre, the oldest of the three, had a sharp mind and inquisitive nature. He was also boisterous, impulsive, and often very silly.

Ignoring Elizabeth, he continued buzzing an apple slice through the air like an airplane. "How big the plane was that brings you and Mademoiselle Jessica from America?" he asked.

"Pierre," Elizabeth said, making it sound like a warning. He looked at her with a wide-eyed, innocent expression that didn't fool her for an instant. "Put the apple on your plate or in your mouth," she told him.

His five-year-old sister Claudine pushed back

her long brown curls and held a banana up to her eye like a telescope. *"L'aéroplane est très grand, n'est pas?"*

"Can you ask me if the plane was very large in English?" Elizabeth asked. The children were supposed to practice their English by speaking it with Elizabeth and Jessica at all times. "And please take the banana out of your eye," Elizabeth ordered.

Claudine giggled and shifted the banana to her nose. "Maybe your airplane, it is so grand like an elephant?"

The youngest, three-year-old Manon, began to clap and bounce in her seat. "I want the book of the elephant!" she cried, referring to the story Elizabeth had read to them at least a thousand times already that week.

Elizabeth sighed wearily. "There will be no elephant book, or any other story, until you three learn not to play with your food during meals," she told them.

According to *The Baby-sitters' Guide,* which she'd recently read, the best way to teach children how to behave properly was to take away privileges. So far the book's advice hadn't proved to be much help, but to Elizabeth's amazement, Pierre and Claudine immediately put their fruit back down on their plates. "That's better," Elizabeth praised them.

"But when the meal is finished, then we can play with our food, yes?" Claudine asked.

"No, you may not," Elizabeth replied, exasperated. From the corner of her eye she noticed Manon beginning to raise a croissant in the air. Elizabeth glared at her, and Manon bit into the pastry instead, dripping strawberry filling down her chin.

How am I going to last until noon? Elizabeth wondered.

Brigitte, one of the maids, came into the nursery. Tall, with short dark hair and a friendly smile, she appeared to be only a few years older than the twins. *"Bonjour,"* she said cheerfully, greeting them with the French version of "good morning." "I come to clear the dishes, but everyone still eats?"

"Just give us a few more minutes," Elizabeth said.

"I shall wait," Brigitte replied. "I must apologize for the rude way I addressed you yesterday, Elizabeth. With the preparation for the party and so many people in the kitchen . . ." She shuddered.

Elizabeth frowned. "I don't know what you're talking about."

"When you were feeding the children their dinner," Brigitte said.

Elizabeth shook her head. "It wasn't me. Jessica had the children last night." She smiled to herself, recalling where *she* had been during that time . . . and with *whom.*

"Then I will apologize to Jessica." Brigitte plunked herself down on the couch and crossed her legs. "Later I will apologize. For now I sit too comfortable. Don't hurry your breakfast," she added with a laugh.

Elizabeth was pleased to have some grown-up company. "Do you work for the de Sainte-Maries all year round?" she asked.

"No, only during my holidays from university," Brigitte replied. "This is my second summer here at Château d'Amour Inconnu."

Elizabeth stopped Pierre from grabbing the heavy ceramic milk pitcher. "I'll pour it," she told him. After she'd refilled his glass, the girls demanded more milk too.

"Your job, it is much harder than mine," Brigitte remarked.

Elizabeth rolled her eyes. "You have *no* idea," she said, fluffing Manon's mop of brown curls. "These guys keep me hopping, running, jumping, and completely twisted in knots."

"Twisted in knots?" Claudine piped up excitedly. "Is it a new game?"

Elizabeth and Brigitte laughed. Suddenly Brigitte's jaw dropped and the color drained from her face as she stared at something across the room.

Startled by the maid's reaction, Elizabeth turned around, half expecting to see a ghost hovering in the doorway. But instead she saw that Laurent had entered the nursery and was creeping up to the table, his eyes wide with mischief, his finger pressed against his lips for silence.

"Laurie!" the children yelled wildly, scrambling to get out of their chairs and run to him. It was obvious they adored their older half brother.

"I wanted to surprise you," Laurent said to the children, laughing as he hugged all three of them at once.

Brigitte, who had jumped to her feet, bowed her head and curtsied, then scrambled out of the room.

How ridiculous! Elizabeth thought. The servants seemed to view Laurent and his family as being on a par with minor deities. That attitude might have been understandable a thousand years ago, when a prince or princess could have had a person's head chopped off, but it seemed terribly silly in modern times . . . especially for a college student like Brigitte.

Haven't these people ever heard of social equality? Elizabeth wondered hotly. *What was the French Revolution all about anyway?*

But the instant Laurent's eyes met hers, Elizabeth's heart leaped, her throat went dry, and all thoughts of history and social studies flew out of her mind.

Laurent shifted uncomfortably, embarrassed by the maid's reaction and quick departure. *I'm a human being!* he had wanted to scream at her. Sometimes he felt as if his parents and their household were stuck in the Middle Ages. And it bothered him.

But Elizabeth's beautiful smile immediately lightened his mood. It hardly seemed possible that a girl so lovely could exist outside of his dreams. "*Bonjour,* Elizabeth," he said softly.

"*Bonjour,* Laurent," she replied.

"Are you going to eat with us?" Claudine asked, jumping up and down at his side with Pierre and Manon.

Laurent gently tweaked her nose, then scooped Manon up into his arms. "If my three little pigs haven't gobbled down every last crumb, I will."

Pierre and Claudine cheered. Manon threw her arms around his neck and gave him a sticky strawberry kiss on the side of his face. Elizabeth pulled up a chair for him.

When the children were settled back into their seats, Claudine turned to him with a serious expression. "Laurie, you can't play with your food until after you finish your breakfast," she warned him.

Laurent narrowed his eyes, bemused.

"It's Mademoiselle Elizabeth's *rule*," Pierre explained, shrugging with his hands palm up at his sides. "We don't understand it either!"

"Well, if it's her rule, I will try to resist the temptation," Laurent said, grinning at her. "We should all do whatever we can to make Elizabeth happy."

Elizabeth blushed a delightful shade of rose. "Thanks," she replied.

Laurent couldn't stop looking at her. Her eyes were the color of the Mediterranean, and her lips looked as soft as the skin of a ripe peach. But Elizabeth was more than beautiful. Sharing breakfast with her felt perfectly natural, as if they'd known each other for *years*.

"Later we will play a game to twist Elizabeth *en

knots!" Claudine interjected. "She told us."

Elizabeth laughed. "I certainly did not," she countered. "And I never said you could play with your food after breakfast."

The children responded with a chorus of groans. Chuckling, Laurent sat back and watched Elizabeth's interaction with his siblings. Her kindness and warmth radiated outward and shone in the way she treated the little ones. She was firm with them but gentle at the same time. And it was obvious to him that they adored her.

Suddenly Manon reached for another croissant and accidentally knocked a glass off the table. Laurent reached down to pick it up, thankful that it had been empty and that it was made of plastic.

"Welcome to the nursery, Laurent," Elizabeth said wryly. "Where life is never boring."

"And rarely it is sane," Laurent added jokingly. "I have an idea, kids. Let's pretend we are all grown-up and have perfect table manners."

Claudine shook her head, pursing her lips. "We're not allowed to play at breakfast."

Laurent and Elizabeth turned to each other and burst out laughing. At that moment he realized that he felt closer to her than to any other girl he'd known. None of the daughters of the nobility that his parents considered suitable for him could melt his heart the way Elizabeth did.

If only I were free, Laurent thought wistfully.

     ❖   ❖   ❖

Standing in front of the antique mirror that hung above her bureau, Jessica placed her hand on her hip and raised her chin, striking a pose. *Perfect,* she thought, pleased with her reflection. After having tried on dozens of outfits, she'd finally settled on a short blue skirt, topped with a flowing, multicolored silk tunic. For an extra touch of elegance she had put on the diamond earrings her grandmother had given her.

Jessica felt an odd shiver as she watched them sparkling in her ears. Earlier that year she had lost one of the earrings. Then, a few nights later, it had mysteriously reappeared on her windowsill. Painful, frightening memories of that time hovered in the back of Jessica's mind.

"No!" she said, squeezing her eyes shut as she forced the images away. Back then her life had been filled with death and obsession. But she'd survived.

Jessica gripped the edges of the tiny bureau and drew in a deep gulp of air. She refused to let the past spoil the romantic adventure she was having with Jacques. With fierce determination she turned her attention back to the present.

Her hands trembled only slightly as she rummaged through the odds and ends strewn across her dresser, picking through her selection of cosmetics. "Mauve Madness?" she wondered as she uncapped a tube of lipstick. Grimacing, she closed it and tossed it aside.

"I must have been crazy to buy such an ugly

shade," she muttered. She found another more to her liking called Strawberry Sundae and smoothed a generous layer across her lips.

Finally Jessica was ready. "This is it," she whispered to her reflection, her eyes shimmering with excitement. She couldn't wait to see everyone's reaction when she introduced her new boyfriend, the duke-to-be of Norveaux. *Things are going to change around here,* she thought. *Good-bye, "Jessica, the lowly servant." Hello, "Miss Wakefield, the honored guest."*

Giggling, she made her way to the door, absently stepping over piles of discarded clothing on the floor.

In the hallway Jacques was leaning against the wall with his arms folded. "At last," he muttered.

Jessica's eyes narrowed slightly at the petulant tone in his voice. "Aren't I worth waiting for?" she asked sharply.

Jacques rushed over to her and enveloped her in a huge hug. "Of course you are, *mon ange,*" he told her. "It's just that I care for you so deeply . . . I lose all my patience when we are apart." He touched his lips to hers and whispered, *"Je t'aime."*

Jessica sighed contentedly. She'd picked up enough French in her classes at Sweet Valley High and around the château to understand those words. "I love you too," she replied.

He kissed her fully, and Jessica felt as if a million sparks of brilliant light were cascading over her and Jacques.

Afterward she leaned back and smiled up at him. "I suppose I should touch up my lipstick before we go downstairs to breakfast."

Jacques's eyes became clouded. Jessica giggled, presuming the reason for his troubled look. "I won't take more than ten seconds this time. I promise," she assured him.

"We need to talk," he said flatly.

Jessica shrugged out of his arms and opened the door to her room. "In ten seconds we'll talk. First I have to put on more lipstick."

"No, Jessica." He followed her into the room and shut the door behind him. "*First* we will talk."

Hands on her hips, Jessica glared at him. She didn't care how gorgeous and sexy he was—he didn't have the right to order her around. "I don't remember inviting you in here," she said.

"You must hear me out," Jacques pleaded.

"You're in no position to tell me what I *must* do," she retorted hotly. "Now if you don't mind . . ."

Jacques rubbed his hand over his face and exhaled loudly. "You're absolutely right," he admitted. "I don't know what gets into me sometimes. But the thing is . . . I can't be seen here with you."

"What?" Jessica gasped incredulously. How was she going to show off her royal boyfriend to the de Sainte-Maries if he refused to be seen with her? All her plans for the summer would be ruined!

A cold suspicion began to take shape in her gut. "Why, Jacques?" she demanded. "Because you're a noble heir and I'm not? Is that what this is about?"

Jacques shook his head emphatically. "No, of course not. That would never stand in the way of my feelings for you. But there is another reason."

Jessica tapped her foot impatiently. "I'd love to hear it."

"It's about the family . . . ," he said, hesitating.

"Whose family—yours or mine?" she asked tersely.

Jacques pushed his hand through his hair and rocked back on his heels. "The others . . . the other family."

Jessica frowned, confused. "The de Sainte-Maries?"

Jacques nodded. "That's correct," he replied. "The de Sainte-Maries. I can't be seen with you because of the de Sainte-Maries. . . . I can't allow them to see *me*."

Jessica sat down on the edge of her bed. "You don't think the prince and princess would welcome you?"

"Welcome me?" Jacques choked out an incredulous laugh. "They would sic their wild dogs on me and allow my body to be torn to shreds!"

Jessica stared at him for a long moment, wondering whether or not to believe him. She hadn't seen any wild dogs on the de Sainte-Maries' property. But the vulnerable look in Jacques's eyes tugged at her heart.

Jacques lowered himself on one knee before her, as if he were proposing marriage in one of those sappy old black-and-white movies her twin loved to watch. "*Ma chèrie,* will you at least listen to me before you cast me aside?" be begged.

Jessica pressed her lips together tightly to keep from giggling at his melodramatic action.

"The de Sainte-Marie family and mine are sworn enemies," he explained. "They've been locked in a feud with each other over a land dispute since the fourteenth century. You would lose your job if they found out about me." He reached up and squeezed her hand. "I wish I might make the peace with *les* de Sainte-Maries. But if I even try, my father, he would, how you say, *disown* me."

Crestfallen, Jessica sighed. "We can't have your father disowning you," she said. "And I don't want to be shipped back to Sweet Valley just yet." She smiled sadly. "It seems we'll have to keep our relationship a secret."

Jacques got off his knees and sat down beside her. "It's the only way," he agreed.

Jessica rested her head on his shoulder. "It's sort of romantic," she said, trying to get used to the idea. She wasn't going to spend the rest of her summer as a pampered guest of the royal family. *But I'll be sneaking off to meet the hottest-looking guy in France,* she reminded herself. *And someday Jacques will become the duke of Norveaux. . . .*

As he kissed her again, Jessica imagined herself as the duchess of Norveaux, living in a place even more spectacular than the Château d'Amour Inconnu. *Meeting Jacques was a dream come true,* she thought.

"I'm thankful that you understand," Jacques whispered.

Jessica recalled the story Jacques had told her about the secret lovers who'd lived on the island hundreds of years ago and whose tale had given the Château d'Amour Inconnu its name.

According to the legend, Prince Frédéric the Third had fallen hopelessly in love with Isadora, a pretty young maiden with a beautiful voice. But because she wasn't a member of the nobility, they'd had to keep their love a secret.

Jessica crossed her wrists behind Jacques's neck. "We'll be just like Prince Frédéric and Isadora," she said.

Jacques chuckled. "I only hope our story will finish differently."

The legend had a very unhappy ending. Prince Frédéric had been forced to marry another woman of his class. And poor, brokenhearted Isadora had turned into a white dove whose sad song lived forever.

Jessica smiled. "I hope so too," she replied with a giggle. "I can't sing."

Jacques tipped back his head and laughed. *"Tu es comme un rayon de soleil,"* he said.

Before Jessica had a chance to ask him what that meant, he lowered his lips to hers for another incredible, sizzling kiss.

Chapter 3

Jessica hummed to herself as she headed toward the children's outdoor play area later that morning. There was a joyful bounce in her step, and she couldn't stop smiling. Seeing Jacques again had energized her completely, and she was ready for anything—even three rambunctious, pint-size royal terrors.

Elizabeth was pushing Claudine on a deluxe swing set while Pierre and Manon were digging in the sandbox. The children's area was also equipped with a huge, wooden dollhouse in the shape of a castle, a jungle gym, slides, and seesaws. There was also a small shed full of toys and games.

"Mademoiselle Jessica!" the children called, waving to her. Pierre and Manon threw their pails and shovels aside and came running toward her.

Jessica felt a rush of delight at their enthusiastic welcome. They really were three of the cutest little kids she'd ever known. "Hello, *mes amis!*" she sang out cheerfully, greeting everyone as "her friends."

Claudine clamored to get down from the swing, then joined her brother and sister, who were jumping around Jessica like happy puppies. "Will you let us play with our food after lunch?" Pierre asked.

Jessica laughed and turned to Elizabeth. "What's he talking about?" she mouthed.

"Don't ask," Elizabeth quipped, watching her with a narrow-eyed, suspicious look. "What's going on, Jess?"

"Whatever do you mean?" Jessica drawled.

"You're *early*," Elizabeth replied dryly. "That always means something." Jessica's chronic lateness was legendary. She never wore a watch since she held the belief that nothing important would start until she had arrived anyway. "I have a feeling you're up to no good," Elizabeth added.

Jessica crossed her arms and sniffed, trying to appear insulted. "Thanks a lot," she retorted indignantly. Then she burst out giggling.

"Tell me!" Elizabeth demanded.

Jessica grinned and clapped. "Hey, kids, let's see who can swing the highest!" She wasn't sure if they were old enough to understand what she was about to say, but she didn't want to take any chances.

The children immediately scrambled for the swings, squealing enthusiastically. Jessica lifted Manon into a safety swing and fastened the seat belt.

As the twins stood side by side, pushing the

41

kids on the swings, Jessica shared her fabulous news. "Jacques has come to see me!"

Elizabeth stared at her blankly.

"Don't tell me you've forgotten him?" Jessica said. "We met him and his father on the train. . . . Jacques is the guy who helped me with my baggage—"

"Yes, I know who you mean," Elizabeth interrupted flatly.

"I knew he would come and see me," Jessica gushed. "He's such a fabulous guy. . . ." She smiled brightly. "I love him so much, Liz. I really think he's The One."

"Is he staying here at the château?" Elizabeth asked.

"I wish." Jessica pushed Pierre's swing, then stepped over to Manon's. "It would be so fabulous if Jacques could stay here. But he can't because of a problem between his family and the de Sainte-Maries. Some old feud that's been going on for hundreds of years."

"Who's the highest?" Claudine yelled, interrupting the twins' conversation.

"It's a tie," Elizabeth answered blandly.

"Push me the hardest!" Pierre shouted.

"No, me!" Claudine responded. "Push me up to the sun!"

"Up to the sun!" Manon echoed, kicking her legs wildly. Jessica absently noticed that Manon had flung off one of her blue sneakers.

"Jacques told me he'd be in big trouble if the

prince and princess catch him on their property,"
Jessica continued. "But he came to see me in spite
of the risk. . . . Isn't that so romantic?"

"I don't know, Jess," Elizabeth replied carefully. "It
doesn't seem right to go against the de Sainte-Maries
on this issue. After all, the château *is* their home."

Jessica reeled back as if she'd been slapped.
"How can you say that?" she snapped hotly. "Is it
right for them to keep two people who love each
other apart because of some ridiculous old feud?"

Elizabeth turned and gave her a gentle, big-sister
smile. "I just don't want to see you hurt," she explained.

Jessica's expression softened. "I know." But she
wasn't ready to let her twin off the hook completely. Elizabeth had been acting like a bossy
know-it-all ever since they'd left Sweet Valley, and
Jessica was tired of it.

She raised her eyebrows and gave Elizabeth a
pointed look. "But it goes both ways," Jessica said.
"I don't want to see *you* hurt either. Remember,
even a prince can turn into a frog if you kiss him too
much—and he can be a very bad influence on you."

Elizabeth's cheeks turned bright red. "I'm sorry
about last night," she muttered.

"You should be!" Jessica replied. Then she
threw Elizabeth's own words back at her. "Didn't I
already tell you once that I wasn't going to put up
with your *selfish, lazy attitude* this summer?"
Jessica tilted her head and pursed her lips, as if she

were struggling to remember something important. Then she abruptly widened her eyes with
mock astonishment and snapped her fingers.
"That's what *you* told *me*. Ironic, huh?"

"OK, I get your point," Elizabeth conceded. "It
was totally irresponsible of me to ditch you last
night and to force you to cover for me."

Jessica savored the victory over her twin. "Don't
worry, I'll let you make it up to me, Liz. You can
work my shift when Jacques comes back."

"Great," Elizabeth responded flatly. "I'll see
you later . . . at five o'clock sharp."

Jessica smiled. "Say hello to Prince Laurent for
me."

"What makes you think I'm going to see him
this afternoon?" Elizabeth asked.

Jessica flashed her a knowing grin. "Aren't you?"

Elizabeth shrugged. "We haven't made any plans."

"Who's the highest now?" Pierre shouted.

"I think you're all the highest," Jessica responded breezily. Apparently satisfied with that,
the children cheered.

Elizabeth chuckled. "I'll see you guys later," she
said as she turned to go.

"Don't be late again," Jessica called after her.

Elizabeth glanced over her shoulder. "I won't,"
she promised.

Jacques Landeau, Elizabeth groaned to herself
as she walked back to the château. *I thought we*

were rid of that fake charmer. But she knew it would be dangerous to let out her true feelings about Jacques. Any opposition would only make him seem more attractive to Jessica.

Elizabeth felt suddenly exhausted . . . and *hungry.* She realized she hadn't eaten much at breakfast, first because the kids had been behaving so outrageously. Then Laurent had arrived, and she'd totally forgotten about food. Elizabeth sighed, remembering how thrilled she'd felt sitting with him at the table. . . . *But even girls in love have to eat,* she reminded herself.

The kitchen was in the final stages of its Saturday scrub down when Elizabeth entered. At the table where the children usually took their meals, three maids were polishing silverware. Other workers were wiping down the appliances, hanging clean curtains, or replacing the newly washed glass fixtures on the lights around the room.

Fernand, the head cook, eyed Elizabeth sharply. *"Il n'est pas l'heure du repas,"* he grumbled, telling her it wasn't mealtime.

"Yes, I know," Elizabeth replied. "I thought I might make myself a sandwich or something if it's OK."

The chef let out a stream of French words, this time too rapidly for Elizabeth to understand. She suspected what he said wasn't complimentary, especially when several people turned to her and sniggered.

One of the maids polishing the silver apparently took pity on her. "The prince and princess have taken their guests to a restaurant off the island," she explained. "The children will have . . . how do you say? *Old* things."

"You mean leftovers?" Elizabeth asked.

"*Oui* . . . yes. Leftovers," the maid said, smiling brightly as she wiped her hands on a towel. "Because you help me with my English, I will assist you now."

A short time later Elizabeth left the kitchen loaded down with a basket of chicken sandwiches, red plums, green grapes, assorted pastries, and a large bottle of orange seltzer. *I'll never be able to finish all this*, she thought. She'd tried telling that to the maid, but the woman had replied that taking care of the de Sainte-Marie children required lots of strength. "You eat to keep the energy up," she had insisted.

Chuckling to herself, Elizabeth went outdoors to find a quiet, shady spot where she could enjoy her lunch in peace. The grounds around the château were covered with lush green lawns and patches of brightly colored flowers, and the day was just too perfect to stay inside.

Elizabeth meandered into the wild English garden. Clusters of red and yellow tulips lined the sides of the white stone path. When she came to a fork in the path, Elizabeth turned right. After a few minutes she realized she was heading toward the stables. *I wonder if anyone would mind if I took Cendrillon out for a ride,* she thought. She decided to find one of the workers and ask.

Elizabeth approached the largest of three white

barns and pushed open the door. Just then she heard her name called from behind. She whirled around and saw Laurent coming from one of the other barns. Watching him walk toward her, Elizabeth felt a warm sensation of pleasure. He was wearing faded blue jeans and a black T-shirt that showed off his lean, rugged build. *He's totally gorgeous!* Elizabeth thought.

"You're here," Laurent said, obviously surprised to see her.

Elizabeth lowered her gaze, suddenly self-conscious. *What if he thinks I'm chasing him too much?* she worried. "I just came to see if I could . . . if Cendrillon . . ." Elizabeth swallowed hard. "If this is a bad time . . ."

He drew her into his arms. "It's *perfect.*"

"You're sure?" Elizabeth glanced up at him hopefully.

Laurent's deep blue eyes shimmered with a look of happiness as he gazed at her. "I've just instructed my groom to saddle up Pardaillan and Cendrillon," he explained. "In a few minutes I would have been on my way to find *you.*" He gently touched the side of her face. "But what else could I expect from the girl of my dreams?"

A sweet, warm glow spread through Elizabeth's body. "Um . . . how about lunch?" she replied, holding up the wicker basket. "I probably have enough here to feed us *and* the horses."

Laurent chuckled. "Wonderful!"

Just then the groom brought out the white stallion and the black mare. "Are you happy to see me?" Elizabeth cooed to Cendrillon as she stroked the horse's neck. The animal whinnied and tapped its hoof.

Laurent laughed. "I didn't know she understood English."

The air was rich with the scent of damp earth and leaves as Elizabeth followed Laurent along a trail that meandered through the de Sainte-Marie forest. Sunbeams cut through openings between the trees, shimmering on a bubbling brook that ran parallel to the trail. *I'm riding through the enchanted forest,* Elizabeth marveled.

They came to a clearing and stopped for lunch. The area was dotted with bushes of lavender, and a natural dam had created a pond of crystal clear water. "This is beautiful!" Elizabeth exclaimed as she dismounted.

Laurent grinned. "I'm glad you like it," he replied.

As he led the horses over to the water for a cooling drink Elizabeth looked around for a good picnic spot. She noticed a wide, rectangular stone protruding from the ground near the pool. She draped her jacket over the stone for a tablecloth and set out the contents of her basket. On impulse she gathered a fragrant cluster of lavender blossoms for a centerpiece. Everything was ready by the time Laurent finished watering the horses.

"I didn't know we were dining formally this

afternoon," Laurent teased as he sat down across from her.

"That's all right," Elizabeth responded with a smile. "Just be sure to leave the waitress a big tip."

Bracing his hands on the edge of the rock, Laurent leaned toward her until his lips hovered close to hers. "Of course," he whispered. "The service here"—he kissed her softly—"is excellent."

Elizabeth kissed him back. "I'm glad you like it, Your Highness."

He chuckled at that. "I do."

They devoured the chicken sandwiches—which were delicious—then moved on to the assorted pastries. Elizabeth selected an éclair and nearly swooned at the first bite. She closed her eyes and chewed slowly to savor the rich, creamy flavor.

When she opened her eyes again, Laurent was watching her with an amused expression. "I take it you like that?"

Elizabeth laughed. "How could you tell?"

"*J'ai deviné* . . . a lucky guess," he replied jokingly.

After lunch they packed up the debris in the wicker basket. A cool breeze rustled through the trees. Elizabeth shook out her jacket and draped it around her shoulders. "Do you come to this spot often?" she asked Laurent as they sat side by side on the rock.

"I did when I was a child," he told her. "I used to play here by myself for hours."

"Was it lonely?" Elizabeth asked softly.

Laurent chuckled. "It was great fun," he countered. "I would pretend I was an American cowboy, and this rock where we sit now was a stagecoach. It was my job to shoot all the robbers that came near it. My parents would allow no toy guns, so I had to use a twig."

Elizabeth smiled. The image of Laurent as a little boy tugged at her heart. She could picture him playing, his blue eyes wild with excitement, wielding his "weapon" with fierce determination. "Did you also make those funny sound effects when you took your shots at the robbers?" she teased.

Laurent raised his eyebrows. "Of course." Elizabeth laughed as he demonstrated his skill at making the sound of a gunshot. "I also had an imaginary sidekick named François," he added. "François was supposed to cover me, but I usually wound up saving him."

Elizabeth playfully tugged the collar of his T-shirt. "What a hero!"

Laurent gave her a crooked smile. "I can't believe I'm telling you all this. I've never told anyone."

"I'm honored," Elizabeth responded, hugging his arm.

"What about you?" he asked. "Did you have the imaginary friends when you were growing up?"

Elizabeth thought back to her childhood. "No, I just had Jessica," she replied. "She was enough!"

They laughed. Laurent reached for her hand and laced his fingers through hers. "You're more than a

50

dream come true, Elizabeth. You're a miracle."

Elizabeth rested her head on his shoulder. She felt totally at peace, yet excited and alive. *If only this moment could last forever,* she wished. But she realized it wasn't just that one moment that was so spectacular; *every* moment with Laurent was special. Elizabeth could almost imagine a future with him. . . .

"So deep in thought," Laurent remarked. He gently brushed his lips across her forehead.

Elizabeth sighed dreamily. "What's it like, being a prince?"

"My life is like anyone's—some parts of it are good, and some are not so good," he told her.

Elizabeth absently ran her finger over the rough surface of the stone as she considered his response. "Tell me about it," she said.

"Let's see. . . ." Laurent wrapped his arm around her, drawing her closer to his side. "The thing that is worse about being a member of a royal family is that people consider me often as an *institution* rather than a human being. They fawn all over me or jump around nervously . . . without ever looking me in the eye."

"That would be difficult for me to deal with," Elizabeth replied.

"You never treated me like a royal," he said. "I love that most about you, Elizabeth."

"You never treated me like a peon," she remarked.

Laurent nodded smugly. "That's right. Our first meal together, I cooked. And if you have time now,

I'll serve you a cup of the very best coffee in the world. My cottage is only a short distance from here."

Elizabeth glanced at her watch. She had nearly an hour before she had to take over from Jessica. "I'd love coffee," she said.

Hand in hand, they walked over to the shady spot near the pool where the horses were standing. "There are advantages to being a prince," he said, grinning. "I have an awesome horse."

Pardaillan raised his head and flicked his tail, as if in response to Laurent's compliment.

Elizabeth chuckled. "Cendrillon is just as awesome," she said, patting the mare.

"Oh, close, maybe," Laurent joked.

"What else is good about being a prince?" Elizabeth asked Laurent as they rode along the trail at a leisurely pace.

Laurent turned to her and laughed. "Isn't Pardaillan enough?"

Elizabeth scowled in response.

"OK, OK, let's see. . . . For one thing, my family's power and prestige makes it possible for me to influence social changes . . . and to help others on a grand scale," Laurent continued. "I uphold the traditions and dignity of my people."

"I'm sure you're a wonderful leader," Elizabeth responded, smiling broadly. She leaned over and kissed him. "You're a wonderful *person*."

Laurent's mood seemed to darken suddenly, and a brooding look came into eyes. "I wonder if you'd still think that if you knew . . ." His voice trailed off.

Elizabeth shifted uneasily. "What do you mean? If I knew *what*?"

Laurent glanced away. Then, just as suddenly, he flashed her a huge smile. "Enough of this serious talk," he said. "I'll race you to the cottage!"

"You're on!" Elizabeth replied, urging Cendrillon to gallop. They rode like the wind, through the forest and across a wide meadow. From the corner of her eye she saw Laurent pulling ahead of her. "We can't let them beat us, Cendrillon!" she shouted.

Elizabeth laughed joyfully as the world seemed to rush by her in a streak of bright colors. She felt as if her heart were pounding as fast and as hard as Cendrillon's hooves. Finally Laurent's cottage appeared in the distance. The horses were side by side until the very end, when Cendrillon inched ahead. Elizabeth won the race by a nose.

She climbed off the mare and, whooping victoriously, jumped up and down. Laurent sauntered over to her with a wry grin on his face. "Congratulations," he muttered.

"Thanks, I deserve it!" she replied smugly. "Cendrillon and I were great, weren't we?"

"And you are so modest," he teased.

Elizabeth's stomach fluttered as Laurent took her into his arms. He kissed her slowly and deeply, as if they had all the time in the world to be together. Elizabeth's heart melted. Losing herself in the glorious sensations swirling through her, she clung to Laurent.

When the kiss ended, Elizabeth drew in a shaky breath. "Mmm, was that for winning the race?" she whispered, her arms still wrapped around his neck.

Laurent touched his forehead to hers and smiled. "No, that's my consolation prize for losing. This one is yours for winning. . . ." Then he lowered his lips to hers for another searing, passionate kiss.

Wonderful tingles coursed through Elizabeth's body. After a moment she broke off the kiss and pressed her lips against Laurent's neck, breathing in his delicious, masculine scent. She hadn't felt such strong emotions for a guy since . . . *Todd.*

A strong pang of guilt shot through Elizabeth, and she squeezed her eyes shut tightly for a moment, willing herself not to think about Todd. There was no reason she should feel guilty for kissing Laurent. Todd had broken up with *her.*

Still, Elizabeth thought, resting her head on Laurent's shoulder, *Todd could've at least written me a letter. Maybe there'll be a letter waiting when I get back to the château—*

With a wince Elizabeth forcibly derailed that train of thought. Laurent was here with her now, and *he* was the one who was making her heart sing.

Elizabeth gave Laurent a squeeze, and he gently hugged her back. Then he planted a soft kiss on the top of her head.

Todd is history, Elizabeth thought solemnly.

Chapter 4

I can't believe she's doing this to me again! Jessica raged silently as she glanced at the wall clock in the nursery. Elizabeth was nearly two hours late, the children had grown tired and cranky, and Jessica's nerves were stretched to the limit.

Pierre dropped a book on her lap. "Read it to us," he demanded.

"No," Claudine shrieked, running toward Jessica with another book. She pushed Pierre aside. He shoved her back, knocking her to the floor. Claudine let out a loud wail and threw her book at his head. Then Pierre starting crying too.

Jessica cast a stern look at Pierre and Claudine. "Sit on the couch and be quiet," she ordered. Suddenly a wooden block came whizzing by, narrowly missing Jessica's head. "What the—" She whipped her head around just in time to see

Manon ducking behind a huge stuffed rabbit.

I'm going to kill *Elizabeth,* Jessica fumed.

Just then she heard footsteps approaching from the hall. "Prepare to die, Liz!" Jessica grumbled under her breath, presuming it was her wayward twin.

But it was Anna, the housekeeper, who appeared at the door. In her midthirties, she was tall and slim, with brown eyes and long brown hair she wore tied back at the nape of her neck. A few dark freckles were scattered across her nose and cheeks. "I've brought your mail," she said, handing two envelopes to Jessica.

They were both addressed to her twin, one from Enid Rollins and one from Maria Slater. Smirking, Jessica tossed them on the table. *Of course Elizabeth's boring friends would have plenty of time to write to her,* she thought.

"Are the children behaving today?" Anna asked.

"Oui!" they answered in unison. "We're being very nice." As if to demonstrate, they all ran over to the doll corner and began playing quietly.

Suddenly Elizabeth burst in, red faced and breathless. "I am *so* sorry I'm late. I lost track of time. . . . Hi, Anna," she said, glancing at the housekeeper. Then she turned to Jessica with a pleading look in her eyes. "I ran all the way back from the stables. I hope you're not mad, Jess."

Jessica clenched her teeth, anxious to tell her sister exactly *how* mad she was. But she didn't want to do it in front of Anna.

56

"Is this today's mail?" Elizabeth inquired as she went over to the table.

"Yes, I just brought it up," Anna replied, turning to leave. "And now I must go check on the evening's meal. You may bring the children down to the kitchen in twenty minutes."

After Anna left, Jessica took a deep breath and prepared to pounce. "Elizabeth—," she began, her voice as cold as steel.

Her twin looked up with a sad, confused expression on her face. "Is this all there was for us? Nothing else?"

Jessica glared at her, seething. "Who cares about the mail?"

Elizabeth shrugged. "I just thought maybe Todd . . ." She pressed her bottom lip between her teeth, and a wistful look flickered in her eyes. Then Elizabeth shook her head, as if to clear it. "Oh, it doesn't matter," she said.

She was hoping to hear from Todd, Jessica realized. The harsh words she'd been gathering died in her throat, and her gut twisted with guilt. The truth was, Todd *had* sent Elizabeth a letter the previous week, which Jessica had intercepted. It had arrived in the aftermath of the twins' huge fight, when they still weren't speaking to each other. Furious at Elizabeth, Jessica had secretly destroyed Todd's letter.

But isn't Elizabeth better off without him? Jessica reasoned. After all, Laurent was a thousand times better. Then another pesky twinge nagged her. *What if it doesn't work out with Laurent either?*

Jessica had heard a rumor that Laurent and the countess's daughter, Antonia, were supposed to be getting together that summer. She hadn't mentioned it to Elizabeth at the time because it hadn't seemed important. But now that her sister seemed to be falling for the prince . . .

Jessica absently stared into space, trying to sort out the pieces. *Just the idea of stealing another girl's boyfriend would horrify Elizabeth, so I can't tell her about Laurent and Antonia,* she decided. Her twin would give up without a fight and let that nasty little witch take the prince.

Maybe I should just tell her about Todd's letter, Jessica thought. *Elizabeth will be angry about it, but she'll forgive me like she always does . . . won't she?*

Jessica nervously chewed the inside of her bottom lip as she hesitated. She didn't want to get into another fight, especially now that she was counting on her twin to cover for her when Jacques was around. *Besides, Todd will probably write again,* she assured herself.

"I really am sorry about being late," Elizabeth said, cutting into Jessica's thoughts.

Jessica shrugged and put on a cheerful grin. "No problem," she responded, trying to soothe her own guilty conscience. "But you're awfully sweaty." She sniffed loudly and wrinkled her nose. "And you smell horsey."

Elizabeth nodded. "We went riding."

"I'll stay here and watch the kids if you want to run upstairs for a quick shower," Jessica offered.

"Are you sure?" Elizabeth asked warily.

Jessica shrugged. "Of course, or I wouldn't have said it. But you'd better be back before it's time to take them to dinner," she added.

"I will," Elizabeth replied, bolting for the door. "Thanks, Jess. You're the best."

Again Jessica felt a pang of guilt for not being totally honest with Elizabeth. *It's for her own good,* Jessica reassured herself. *Besides, Todd Wilkins is a total drip. Elizabeth doesn't need him—she has a bona fide prince in her life now. And I* know *she can win him away from Antonia!*

Elizabeth wiped her hand across her sweaty forehead as she hurried toward the back staircase that led to her room in the servants' wing. She appreciated her twin's offer to watch the kids for a few more minutes while she showered and changed, although she was a bit concerned about the reason for Jessica's sudden generosity. *She's either going to try to manipulate me into doing something I don't want to do, or she's hiding something,* Elizabeth thought.

As she crossed the wide corridor at the end of the hall Elizabeth caught sight of Countess di Rimini and her daughter, Antonia, in the formal parlor. The countess was a tall, striking woman with bright red hair, piercing green eyes, and a permanent scowl on her face. Antonia was a younger copy of her mother, with fewer wrinkles around her mouth. Both women were perched side by side on an eighteenth-century red velvet divan, sipping tea from dainty china cups.

"Those American girls are never working," Elizabeth overheard the countess hiss in a stage whisper.

"What do you expect from common servants?" Antonia responded.

Elizabeth's blood boiled, but she walked by with her head held high. *Why don't they mind their own business?* she thought. Clenching her fists at her side, Elizabeth headed quickly for the staircase. But she wasn't fast enough.

She heard the click-clacking sound of high-heeled footsteps on the polished wood floor behind her. "Now what?" Elizabeth muttered to herself as she turned around.

Antonia stood there, with her arms folded and her nose in the air, glaring at Elizabeth.

"Is there something you wanted?" Elizabeth asked, forcing an even, neutral tone into her voice.

"You are a servant to the de Sainte-Maries, so don't think you can charm your way out of your work here," Antonia warned.

Elizabeth blinked, taken aback by her rudeness. "I don't know what you're talking about. I take my duties as an au pair *very* seriously."

"Where are the children now?" Antonia

snapped. "You haven't left them alone, have you?"

Elizabeth gripped the ornately carved post on the banister and exhaled slowly, fighting to maintain control. "They're in the nursery, with my sister," she explained tightly. "Now if you'll excuse me, I'm in a bit of a rush—"

"Not so fast!" Antonia's lips twisted into a cruel, haughty smile. "Let me give you some advice. Perhaps in America family honor isn't important, but here in Europe it's *crucial*. And you must face it—you don't have the noble breeding necessary to rise above your station."

Something inside Elizabeth snapped. "You're right, Antonia. In America all of us are equal. We only keep breeding records for *animals*." With that she whirled around and rushed up the stairs.

"I would be careful if I were you!" Antonia called after her. "It's when you're standing next to nobility that you look your shabbiest!"

Elizabeth cringed but continued on her way without a backward glance. *I despise that girl!* she raged silently as she stormed into her room. She slapped her fist against her palm, wishing she could do the same to Antonia's face. *And I despise her mother too!*

"But I can't let them get to me," Elizabeth grumbled as she paced the length of her room. Fuming about the di Riminis was a total waste of energy and time. She reminded herself that she had a job to do, and if she didn't hurry up and get in the shower, she'd be late—*again*. Then Jessica's unexpected generosity would vanish as mysteriously as it had appeared

Elizabeth went over to her dresser and took out a clean outfit: blue jeans and a soft-green cotton sweater. She had exactly twelve minutes left to shower, change, and report to the nursery.

The di Riminis' narrow-minded view of the world was their own problem. *Thank goodness Laurent doesn't share their attitude*, Elizabeth thought.

Jessica was thrilled when Jacques came to see her again the following evening. It was just after sunset, and the sky was streaked with purple and red as they took a romantic stroll in the rose garden. The gardeners and servants didn't work on Sundays, for which Jessica was thankful. The last thing she'd need was to be spotted with Jacques by one of the de Sainte-Maries' faithful staff. She was equally glad that Prince Nicolas and Princess Catherine were out for the evening, having taken the countess di Rimini and Antonia to the opera.

Jacques picked a white blossom and gently traced a line across Jessica's chin with its soft, fragrant petals. "You are so beautiful, more than this flower," he whispered in a deep, husky voice.

Jessica almost swooned as a warm flush of pleasure rose to her cheeks. "I'm so glad you're here, Jacques."

They sat down on a wrought iron bench under an arbor of crimson roses and snuggled close together. Jacques brushed a gentle kiss across Jessica's lips. *"Je t'aime de tout mon cœur,"* he whispered.

Jessica murmured a sigh. She didn't know what he'd just told her, but she was sure it was something wonderfully romantic.

"Tu es si belle." Jacques kissed her again. *"Tu es aussi delicate qu'une fleur. Tu es aussi jolie qu'un ange."* He leaned back and gazed at her directly, his brown eyes dancing with amusement. "You understand these words I say, yes?"

Jessica smiled dreamily. "Not a clue."

"I teach you, then," Jacques offered.

"Later." Jessica boldly kissed him again.

Jacques chuckled against her lips, then pulled her closer and deepened the kiss. She felt his fingers brushing through her hair, caressing the back of her neck. Jessica shivered with delight.

Suddenly Jacques leaned back. "Are you cold, *ma chérie?*"

Jessica smiled. "Not in the least."

"Ma chérie means 'my dear,'" he explained.

"I actually know that," Jessica replied. "I did sit through several semesters of French class."

Jacques pushed a lock of her hair behind her ear and gazed into her eyes. "And *je t'aime de tout mon cœur* means 'I love you with all my heart.' *Tu es si belle,* this means 'you are so beautiful.' *Tu es aussi delicate qu'une fleur*—you are as delicate as a flower. *Tu es aussi jolie qu'un ange*—you are as lovely as an angel."

Jessica hesitatingly repeated each phrase after Jacques.

"Try rolling your *r*'s a bit more," he instructed. "Last night I told you this—*tu es comme un rayon de soleil.* It means you are like a ray of sunshine."

Jessica leaned closer to him and gazed into his warm brown eyes. "I remember."

Jacques placed a feather-soft kiss on her eyebrow. "Now, I say to you the words in English; you translate into *français.*"

Jessica pursed her lips. "Are we really going to have a French quiz right *now?*" she asked. "Don't we have better things to do?"

Jacques shifted away from her. Facing forward, he rested his arms along the back of the bench. "French, it is a beautiful, romantic language," he said.

"No argument there," Jessica responded, bemused—and irritated—by the sudden chill in his mood. "What's wrong, Jacques?"

He turned to her and smiled. "I wish you could say these words to me in my own language," he whispered.

Jessica narrowed her eyes. "What?"

Jacques ducked his head sheepishly. "It is a foolish whim, I know. But for me it is important that we . . . how you say . . . *communicate* the feelings we have to each other with French words."

"Seems we were communicating just fine a minute ago," Jessica responded sharply. "Without any words at all."

"I have caused you to be angry, haven't I?" Jacques said, his voice filled with concern. "Do you want me to go?"

"No, of course not." Jessica exhaled loudly and reached for his hand. "If it means that much to you . . . OK, I'll memorize your sentences."

Jacques immediately enveloped her in a big hug. "Let's go quickly to your room and get a notebook and pen so you can learn better these words," he suggested.

"What if you get caught?" Jessica argued.

"You said the prince and princess are out for the evening, yes?"

"One of the servants might see us and tell the de Sainte-Maries," Jessica said. She snuggled closer to him on the bench. "Besides, it's nice and cozy here."

Jacques kissed her briefly. "We'll come right back." He stood up and held out his hand to her.

Jessica rolled her eyes. *Obviously I'm not going to talk him out of this,* she realized. Giving in, she placed her hand in his and allowed Jacques to lead her toward the château.

"And when the maiden woke up, she found the bluebird sitting on the highest branch of the weeping tree," Elizabeth read aloud. She sat wedged between Claudine and Pierre on the couch in the nursery, with Manon on her lap.

"The bluebird began to sing a sweet melody," Elizabeth continued. "It was so lovely that all the creatures of the forest came to listen."

Pierre pointed to a squirrel in the corner of the illustration. "Is that the bluebird's friend?"

"It could be," Elizabeth replied as she turned the page. "Suddenly the wicked spell was broken, and the bluebird turned into a handsome prince. The very next day he and the maiden were married. The bells of the palace rang joyfully for all to hear . . . and the prince and princess lived happily ever after."

Elizabeth sighed contentedly. "Happily ever after," she breathed. She couldn't help picturing herself as the princess and Laurent as her handsome prince. *Will our story end happily ever after?* she wondered.

Then she laughed at herself. *Get real!* she thought. She'd known Laurent for only a short time. It was a bit early for wedding plans! Elizabeth closed the book firmly.

"Read it again," Manon protested.

"It's time for bed now," Elizabeth replied. "We can read it again tomorrow. Let's have one big, group hug, and then it's off to dreamland for you three."

They snuggled together noisily for a few seconds, then the children scampered off to the adjoining bedroom. Elizabeth followed to tuck them in. Their mother usually did the honors, but the princess had gone out that evening.

"Good night," Elizabeth whispered after the children had settled down. "Sweet dreams."

"You look like the princess in the book," Claudine said sleepily.

Elizabeth smiled as she turned off the light and slipped out of the room. *Crazy as it seems, I feel like the princess in the book,* she thought.

She'd always imagined that she'd live an ordinary life, in or near Sweet Valley. She'd graduate from Sweet Valley University, then work as a journalist or freelance writer. . . .

Is it possible that I'm destined for another kind of life entirely? Elizabeth wondered. *Could my fairy-tale dreams really come true?*

"Jacques, stop pulling me!" Jessica hissed as they scurried up a rarely used stone staircase in the château. She'd had to run all the way from the rose garden to keep pace with him, but she drew the line at being dragged up the stairs.

"I'm sorry," he said, slowing down a bit. "I just don't want to waste a single minute of our time together."

Jessica sniffed indignantly. "So we're going to spend it on a French lesson?" she grumbled.

When they reached the landing, Jacques flashed her a sexy grin that made her heart turn somersaults. "I love the way you look at this very moment," he declared. "Your face is glowing, and your eyes are shooting silver sparks."

Jessica giggled. "I might shoot *you* if you don't stop acting like we're on our way to an emergency," she teased. "We're here to get a notebook and pen, for Pete's sake."

I don't know if I even have *a notebook,* Jessica thought wryly. But she knew Elizabeth probably had a ton of them.

Moving silently, Jessica and Jacques crept into

the servants' wing and up the stairs to the top floor. "Wait here," Jessica whispered when they reached the door to her twin's room. "I'll just be a minute."

Jacques gripped her elbow and gaped at her with a look of alarm. "This isn't your room," he pointed out urgently.

"It's my sister's," Jessica responded. "Elizabeth is the writer in the family." She slipped through the door, giggling at Jacques's strange reaction. *That guy should learn to relax,* she thought.

Sure enough, Elizabeth had an ample supply of yellow writing pads and sharpened pencils on her desk. Jessica grabbed what she needed and rushed out of the room. But Jacques was nowhere in sight. Then she heard sounds coming from her own room across the hall.

Jessica opened her door, and her jaw dropped. Jacques was on his knees in the middle of her floor, rummaging through a pile of discarded clothing. "What do you think you're doing in here?" she demanded.

Jacques looked up, obviously startled. "I heard someone coming up the stairs, so I ducked in here."

Tucking the notebook under her arm, Jessica pressed her fists against her hips. "And why are you playing with my laundry?"

"I was just going to . . . um . . ." He pushed his fingers through his hair and bit down on his bottom lip. "I want to make a surprise for you, so I was going to fold your clothes."

Jessica stared at him incredulously. "What?"

"I—I wish to prove that I'm a modern guy . . . that I am n-not . . . how you say . . . *male chauvinist*," he stammered.

Jessica studied him for a long moment, noting the sheepish look on his face, the hopeful plea in his eyes. Finally she burst out laughing. "Oh, Jacques! You don't have to clean up after me. Believe me, I'm already impressed—beyond my wildest dreams."

"But I don't mind doing nice things for you," he countered, picking up a black sweater and shaking it out. "You're the kind of girl who deserves to be waited on hand and foot."

Jessica leaned back against her closed door. "I agree with you there, Jacques. And I'm sure someday I'll have lots of servants of my own." *Especially if I become the duchess of Norveaux,* she added to herself.

"Yes, of course you will," he replied. "But for now, why don't we tidy up a bit." He went over to her dresser and began lining up her makeup containers.

"Jacques, you really don't have to do that," Jessica protested.

"I don't mind," he told her.

"Well, I do," she insisted.

"It'll just take a minute. . . . I'll have this whole room in perfect order." He glanced at her. "You can wait for me in the rose garden if you like."

Jessica marched over to him and grabbed his elbows, effectively pulling him away from her dresser. "Come on, Jacques!"

Jacques ducked his head sheepishly. "As you wish," he said. "All I want is to make you happy." He kissed her briefly and smiled. "To the rose garden."

"That's better," Jessica mumbled.

Jacques moved toward the door, then stopped and glanced around the room. "By the way, Jessica, do you still have that piece of costume jewelry I gave you on the train?" He chuckled. "Although I wouldn't blame you if you'd thrown it away. It really wasn't much of a gift."

"Of course I still have it!" Jessica replied emphatically. She went over to her bed and pulled back the pillow to show him. "It gives me sweet dreams."

"Give it back to me," Jacques said.

Jessica replaced the pillow. "No way!"

"Please," he begged. "I'm embarrassed at the cheapness of it. A girl as special and precious as you are deserves a *real* gemstone—not a fake."

"I don't care if it's fake or not," Jessica insisted. "I treasure it because it's from you."

A confused, faraway expression flittered across Jacques's face. "You deserve better," he said softly, his voice heavy with regret.

Deeply touched, Jessica blinked back a sudden tear. "That is so sweet, Jacques." She sighed. "Now let's get out of here."

Monday morning Laurent headed over to the château, a feeling of happiness rising inside him. He couldn't wait to see Elizabeth again. Presuming he'd find her in the nursery with the children, he rushed upstairs. But as he passed the open doorway of his stepmother's sitting room, his father's voice called out to him. *"Entrez, s'il vous plaît,"* Prince Nicolas said, asking Laurent to come in.

Laurent stopped in his tracks and sighed wearily.

Princess Catherine and his father were seated side by side on a green velvet divan near the fireplace. By the serious looks on their faces, Laurent had a pretty good idea of what was about to be discussed. His heart sank as he entered the room and closed the heavy double doors.

Chapter 5

Laurent felt as if the walls of Princess Catherine's sitting room were closing in on him as he paced back and forth like a caged animal. "Father, I have *never* shirked my responsibility to the de Sainte-Marie name," he argued, speaking his words in French. "But you're asking me to give up my entire future. . . ."

Prince Nicolas's expression remained stern. "True, Laurent," he replied, also speaking French. "You've been a blessing to me ever since the day you were born, but you're not a child anymore. The time has come for you to take on a *man's* responsibilities. You are my heir and will one day assume my place as the leader of our people. The name de Sainte-Marie carries both privileges *and* burdens."

"But I'm not ready," Laurent said.

Prince Nicolas waved his hand as if to erase

Laurent's words. "There will be no more discussion. Catherine and I will be hosting an official ball this weekend, and I expect your decision before then."

Laurent inhaled sharply. "This weekend?" he asked incredulously.

"Marriage won't end your life, Laurent," Princess Catherine interjected, favoring her husband with a warm smile. She spoke with the same refined, cultured accent as her husband. "There are those who believe marriage and fatherhood are life's highest blessings."

Laurent gazed beyond them to the three bay windows that looked out over the back of the château. In the distance he could see the edge of the forest where he had taken Elizabeth horseback riding. "Isn't love one of life's blessings?" he asked.

"Duty and love are two sides of the same coin," his father retorted. "A man's honor stems from the love of his family and his people. And in doing his duty, he gives an outward symbol of what is in his heart."

Laurent threw up his hands. "I do honor my family and my heritage," he insisted. "But why must I sacrifice my happiness? What benefit will that bring to the name of de Sainte-Marie?"

His father and stepmother exchanged meaningful looks. "Is there something you aren't revealing?" Prince Nicolas inquired pointedly.

"I've met someone . . . a beautiful girl, with a sharp mind and a kind heart." Laurent took a deep breath, bracing himself. "Her name is Elizabeth Wakefield."

"You can't be serious!" his stepmother uttered.

Prince Nicolas frowned. "Who is she?" he asked his wife. "The name is familiar."

"She's one of my au pair girls, the American twins," Princess Catherine answered.

Prince Nicolas nodded. "Yes, now I remember. They are very lovely girls."

"But they're hardly of a class for Laurent," Princess Catherine countered.

"I love Elizabeth for the person she is," Laurent told them. He turned to his father in desperation.

Prince Nicolas shook his head. "Tradition is wiser than any one man or woman," he said. "Always remember that. You are in a position to secure us a valuable political alliance. There is so much at stake here."

Laurent clenched his fists at his side, frustrated and angry at the situation. He wanted to scream, to pick up one of the priceless figurines on the window shelf and hurl it across the room. But temper tantrums had never been Laurent's style, even when he was a boy.

He looked at the deep lines in his father's face, the love and pride that shone from Prince Nicolas's eyes despite the harshness of his expression. *How can I turn away from my family?* Laurent asked himself. *But how can I live the life that's been chosen for me—a life without Elizabeth?*

Seated at an outdoor table in a seaside café, Jacques scanned the crowd walking by, hoping to catch a glimpse of his father. The old man was more than an hour late, and as the minutes ticked by, a cold panic squeezed Jacques's gut. *Where could he be?* he worried.

He'd nervously shredded his paper napkin and was moving on to the scalloped-edge place mat when he finally spotted his father crossing the street toward the café—with a bikini-clad, blond-haired woman on either arm. Jacques exhaled sharply and rolled his eyes. *When will that man learn to act his age?* he thought hotly.

Jacques rose to his feet as his father led his group over to the table.

"Mesdemoiselles, may I present to you my son, Jacques Landeau," Louis said, opening his arms with a flourish. "These lovely angels are Monique and Carlotta." He spoke in the slow, lilting French typical of natives of the South of France.

Jacques nodded politely, trying to hide his irritation. What he had to say to his father was going to be difficult, and he wanted to get it over with as quickly as possible.

"Enchanté," one of the girls said in a soft, breathy voice, holding out her hand. Jacques wasn't sure if she was Monique or Carlotta—and he didn't care. He absently noticed the bracelet she wore around her narrow wrist. It was made of pearls, not

valuable but with an unusual rosette motif. Jacques reluctantly kissed her hand, then repeated the gesture for her friend.

"Now it's time for me and my son to consult on business," Louis announced cheerfully. "Run along, my beauties."

The girls scampered away, giggling and blowing kisses over their shoulders.

Jacques watched them go, then turned to his father. The smug smile on his tired, wrinkled face tugged at Jacques's heart. Despite his failing health, Louis would always be a rogue.

"You are something else, old man!" Jacques muttered.

Louis Landeau snapped his fingers to signal for a waiter. "I may be old, Jacques—but I'm not *dead*."

"You will be soon if you don't slow down and start taking care of yourself," Jacques said. "Where do you *find* all these women anyway?"

Louis shrugged. "They find *me*."

Jacques laughed aloud, despite the worry and dread weighing heavily on his mind. His father's bouts of coughing and fever had grown much too frequent lately; he'd nearly died of pneumonia the previous winter.

Jacques knew that their current lifestyle, spending their days on the road, had to end soon—before it killed his father. *The old man needs rest and stability, a real home,* he thought. Jacques had made a vow to himself some time ago to provide that home for his father, even though he had no idea how he was going to do it.

"Monique and Carlotta insist on entertaining us for the day on their yacht," Louis said casually after he'd ordered coffee and croissants.

Jacques groaned to himself but said nothing.

His father shot him a pointed look. "What is the matter with you, boy? I find the prettiest girls on the beach and bring them right to you. And this is the thanks I get—nothing but a sour face?" Louis leaned closer and flicked his eyebrows. "Which one is your favorite? I'm partial to Carlotta, but you may have first choice."

"I'm not interested," Jacques replied, silently adding, *because I'm too much in love with Jessica Wakefield.*

Louis threw up his hands. "I will never understand the young!"

"And it seems I'll never understand *you*," Jacques returned.

"*Touché*, my son." Louis slowly stirred sugar into his espresso and raised the demitasse to his lips. "So, how was your weekend?" he asked, eyeing him over the rim.

Jacques cringed. He knew what his father was asking—and he wasn't going to like the answer. "I'm sorry," he replied. "I failed to get the emerald from Jessica."

"What?" Louis lowered the demitasse to the saucer with a loud clink. "Do you mean to say you've spent all this time doing nothing but flirting with the girl?"

"No, of course not," Jacques protested weakly. "I tried to get it, but . . . I just couldn't."

"Try harder!" Louis snapped. "I promised that emerald to one of our best clients. And he's not the kind of man to whom one brings bad news." He pinned Jacques with a sharp look. "Do you understand?"

"Yes," Jacques replied, lowering his eyes.

"This is serious business," his father said. "You can't lose your head over a pretty face right now— especially not *that* one. Trust me, other girls will come along, and soon you won't even remember Jessica's name."

I'll never *forget Jessica,* Jacques silently protested.

Louis smiled gently, all traces of his anger gone. "I'm counting on you, son."

Jacques nodded. "I know. And I won't let you down," he promised. "I'll get that stone one way or another." *Even if it breaks my heart to hurt Jessica.*

"Pierre, it's not polite to speak with your mouth full," Elizabeth told him. Immediately all three children began making singsong, babbling noises while they chewed their lunch. A thick blob of mashed chicken dribbled down Manon's chin and landed on the tray of her high chair.

Elizabeth sighed wearily. They were seated at

the table in a corner of the château's enormous kitchen. The room was pleasantly noisy as the staff prepared the meal that would be served that evening. Pots simmered on the old-fashioned stove, and something that smelled delicious was baking in the oven.

Elizabeth heard someone enter through the back door. Presuming it was Laurent, her heart leaped. She'd kept an eye out for him all morning, almost certain he'd drop in to see her. She turned around expectantly . . . but it was only Anna, the housekeeper, who was coming over to the table.

Elizabeth swallowed her sharp disappointment and smiled politely.

"Good afternoon," Anna said cheerfully.

"We're being very good today," Claudine told her. Pierre and Manon nodded their agreement. Elizabeth rolled her eyes.

"I have good news," Anna announced. "The prince and princess have decided to allow the children to attend the ball on Saturday."

"*Hourra!*" they cheered. Then Claudine ducked her head and giggled. "I mean, *yippee!*" she said, apparently remembering the rule about speaking only English.

"You and your sister will attend also, of course," Anna told Elizabeth.

"Really?" Elizabeth breathed as a quick image of herself dancing with Laurent flashed in her mind's eye. The two of them were swirling gracefully around the ballroom while everyone watched . . . he, handsomely dressed in an official uniform with lots of medals, and she, wearing . . . *jeans?*

Elizabeth blinked, frowning at the ridiculous picture. "I didn't bring anything dressy enough for a formal ball," she admitted.

Anna flicked her hand in a dismissive gesture. "That is nothing," she replied. "In the wardrobe room there are hundreds of gowns. We'll find something suitable, I know."

After the housekeeper left, the children were more rambunctious than ever. Pierre and Manon got into a fight over who could drink the most milk, which resulted in them knocking over their glasses.

"Now you've done it!" Elizabeth snapped, reaching for the dishrag at her side. Experience had taught her always to keep one on hand during meals. *After this summer I'll probably be able to write my* own *baby-sitting guide,* she thought.

"Aren't you happy about going to the ball?" Claudine asked—with her mouth full, of course.

"Sure, I am," Elizabeth replied. "I'm just sad about having to see your food while you're chewing!"

"Sorry," Claudine murmured. She clamped her mouth shut. Pierre and Manon did the same, and for several minutes the children entertained themselves by making silly humming sounds at each other.

The door opened and shut again. Elizabeth

glanced anxiously over her shoulder. This time it was Brigitte the maid who had entered the kitchen.

Elizabeth sighed, her hopes deflating like a brightly colored balloon with a slow leak. *Where are you, Laurent?* she wondered.

I never knew how boring *France could be!* Jessica complained to herself as she stretched out across her bed that night and stared at the swirled pattern in the ceiling. She'd been moping in her room for hours, disappointed that Jacques hadn't bothered to come see her that day. "He'd better have a good excuse," she muttered through clenched teeth.

To make matters worse, the children had been overly excited at dinner, bouncing in their seats like Ping-Pong balls. The entire château was in a frenzy over the upcoming formal ball. "Big deal," Jessica whined.

She flipped over onto her stomach. Bracing her elbows on the mattress, she propped her head up with her fists tucked under her chin. *It stinks that I can't invite Jacques to the ball because of that stupid feud,* she thought.

Just then Jessica's stomach growled hungrily. She and the children had eaten cold sandwiches for dinner while the prince and princess had entertained their guests with a gourmet feast in the dining room.

Jessica smiled slowly. *I'll bet there's lots of*

yummy leftovers, she realized, bolting off her bed. She stuck her bare feet into a pair of sandals and crept downstairs.

The kitchen was deserted at that time of night—and spotless. Jessica padded across the polished floor to the refrigerator and pulled it open. *I was right!* she silently cheered as she examined the contents.

The choice of leftovers was superb. There was baked salmon in what looked like dill sauce, green beans with cream and almonds, artichoke canapés, stuffed olives, black caviar, a huge platter of pâté and cheeses, assorted French pastries. . . . "Now *this* is what I call dinner!" Jessica declared, giggling.

She helped herself to a bit of everything, ending with a rich, custard-filled chocolate éclair. Feeling thoroughly satisfied, she rinsed off her plate and turned off the kitchen light.

Jessica tiptoed up the front staircase, then wished she'd taken another route back to her room when she saw the countess di Rimini in the corridor, heading her way. The scowling woman was wrapped in a yellow chiffon robe trimmed with black feathers.

Maybe if I ignore her, she'll return the favor, Jessica thought. But as they drew closer she saw the dirty look on the countess's face and realized it wasn't going to be a peaceful encounter.

"Just getting in?" the witch inquired coldly. "I would think you'd be ashamed to come in here at all hours, treating your employers' home like a hotel."

Jessica was stunned by the accusation, but she refused to defend herself. She didn't care what the nosy snob thought of her. "My personal life is really none of your business," Jessica retorted.

The countess raised her hand to her chest, her bony white fingers disappearing in the black feathery trim of her robe. "Your manners are deplorable, young lady. But I'm not surprised, considering." She gave Jessica a rude up-and-down glare, then stalked past her toward the stairs.

Jessica's blood was boiling by the time she reached the servants' quarters. She noticed the light shining from under the door of her sister's room and barged in without bothering to knock. "I absolutely can't stand that witch!" Jessica raged.

Elizabeth was sitting up in bed, writing something. "What happened?" she asked.

"That countess *creature!*" Jessica plunked herself down on the bed and drew her knees up to her chin. She recounted what had happened on the stairs. "If I wasn't so afraid of waking everyone up and causing a scene, I would've happily told that ugly witch what I thought of her so-called noble breeding!"

"They certainly are something else. The countess and Antonia make *Bruce Patman* seem humble and down-to-earth," Elizabeth said, comparing the di Riminis to the richest and most arrogant student at Sweet Valley High.

"Jacques isn't like that at all," Jessica pointed out.

Elizabeth lowered her eyes. "Neither is Laurent."

"Speaking of our favorite prince," Jessica began, "what did you guys do this evening while I was stuck feeding sandwiches to the little monsters?"

"I didn't see Laurent today," Elizabeth replied. "I thought I would, but . . ." She shrugged.

Jessica saw the dejected look on her sister's face. "I know how you feel, Liz," she empathized. "Jacques didn't show up today either. Maybe we need to teach these royal blockheads that they can't take the Wakefield twins for granted!"

Elizabeth smiled weakly.

"At least you'll get to be with Laurent at the ball this weekend," Jessica grumbled. "I'll probably have a miserable time, watching everyone else dancing. . . ."

Elizabeth rolled her eyes. "You mean because you're so *shy?*" she responded sarcastically. They both burst out laughing.

"OK, so I might have fun even without Jacques there," Jessica conceded. "But I still wish he were going."

Tuesday afternoon Elizabeth jumped to her feet the instant Jessica walked into the nursery for her shift with the children. "I'm in a bit of a hurry," Elizabeth explained.

"I can see that," Jessica said, smirking. "But don't you understand that it's best to keep the guy waiting?"

"Some other time, Jess," Elizabeth replied tersely. Waving good-bye to the children, she rushed out of the room. After waiting yesterday and all that morning for Laurent to show up, Elizabeth had finally decided to go see him. *I may be living in an old French château for the summer, but I'm still a modern, American girl,* she reminded herself pointedly.

Elizabeth slipped into the bathroom across the hall and checked her appearance in the beveled mirror above the sink. *I guess I'm not too modern to worry about my looks,* she thought wryly.

The glossy, pale rose lipstick Elizabeth had applied that morning was long gone, and her soft dusting of taupe eye shadow was hardly visible. "Maybe I should wear more makeup," she whispered, turning her head from side to side to study the various angles of her face. "How would I look with a more dramatic style, like Jessica's?"

Elizabeth pursed her lips, then wrinkled her nose. *I don't want anyone's style but my own,* she decided.

Laurent would have to accept her as she was— or not at all. But a small, frightened voice in the back of Elizabeth's mind piped up with nagging self-doubts. *What if I really am shabby looking and just don't know it? Maybe that's why Laurent hasn't come to see me for two days. . . .*

"Maybe I should quit letting that nasty Antonia poison my mind with her ridiculous insults!" Elizabeth said under her breath.

She focused her thoughts on seeing Laurent again, and a lush, happy feeling rose in her heart. There was a bounce in her step as she went downstairs.

The household was bustling in preparation for the ball. Extra staff had been hired for the occasion, and workers were dusting and polishing, moving furniture around, steam cleaning the curtains. . . . Elizabeth did her best to sidestep the commotion.

Anna called to her on her way out the back door. "If you plan to go outside, it's better you should bring this," the housekeeper advised, handing Elizabeth a large black umbrella. "It looks like the rain comes soon."

"Thanks," Elizabeth said, tucking the umbrella under her arm.

Anna smiled. "We cannot have you getting soaked and catching the cold just before the big ball. It promises to be one of Château d'Amour Inconnu's most magnificent affairs."

Elizabeth responded with an automatic smile, but all her insecurities suddenly rose up again. She knew it was silly, but she couldn't help the feeling of dread that surrounded her thoughts about the ball. *What if I stand out as a commoner among Laurent's noble friends?* she worried.

Elizabeth's stomach fluttered as if it were filled with nervous butterflies. She was in way over her head, trying to find her way through the strange culture of the nobility without a single clue. *What am I doing, having a romance with a prince?* she wondered.

"You give up, maybe?" Anna asked, cutting through the mental chatter in Elizabeth's head.

"Give up?" Elizabeth echoed, nonplussed.

"Do you decide to stay indoors today?" Anna clarified.

Elizabeth thought for a moment, then gripped the umbrella tightly, steeling her courage. She raised her head high and replied, "Not a chance."

I don't give up easily, Elizabeth added silently.

Chapter 6

Elizabeth felt a rush of pleasure as she approached Laurent's cottage. The rustic scene before her was like an illustration in one of the children's storybooks. Clusters of lavender lined the white stone path to the front door. Daisies and tiger lilies dotted the lawn. To the side of the cottage, a wrought iron bench was nestled under a rose arbor. Elizabeth couldn't imagine a more idyllic and romantic setting.

She was eager to see Laurent again. Being with him made her feel excited, happy, and comfortable all at the same time.

Elizabeth stepped up to the door and knocked firmly. At that very instant a large, cold raindrop splashed down on her wrist. She glanced up at the gray sky. "I guess Anna was right," she said.

When there was no answer, Elizabeth knocked

again. A few more raindrops fell on her. She was just about to open her umbrella when the door finally opened. "Hello, Laurent. It seems I always end up here when it rains," Elizabeth joked.

Laurent hesitated for an instant, as if he might turn her away. Then he flashed her a tight smile. "Come in," he said.

Elizabeth's spirits sagged at his less-than-enthusiastic greeting. Still clutching the umbrella, she nervously rubbed her thumb over the brass handle as she followed Laurent into the sitting room.

A warm, cozy fire blazed in the hearth, but Elizabeth felt chilled. "Did I come at a bad time?" she asked cautiously.

Laurent's gaze shifted away from hers. "I was just going through my mail in the study," he said. "Do you mind if I continue? I'm almost finished."

"I don't mind," Elizabeth replied automatically. "Can I make some coffee?"

"Help yourself," Laurent offered.

Elizabeth chewed her bottom lip as she watched him go. *He doesn't seem too happy to see me today,* she thought. But she refused to let her own insecurities cloud her judgment. *Everyone gets busy and preoccupied once in a while,* she reassured herself. *Even if they're royalty!*

Humming optimistically, Elizabeth went to make the coffee.

The kitchen was small and comfortable, just like the rest of the cottage. The floor was covered in red stone tiles, and the walls were painted a pale green. Potted plants lined the windowsill. Elizabeth recalled the first time she'd been there, the night she'd gotten caught in the storm. Laurent had prepared omelets in the morning. Wearing a white chef's hat, he'd juggled the raw eggs in the air and behind his back. "That's to impress the visiting au pair," he'd said with a wink.

Elizabeth chuckled at the memory as she poured a scoopful of coffee beans into the grinder. It took her a while to figure out how to work the complicated electric coffeemaker, but she finally had two demitasses of steaming, dark espresso prepared. She placed them on a tray that she'd found in a bottom cupboard, then added two linen napkins, the crystal sugar bowl, and two spoons.

Carrying the tray out of the kitchen, Elizabeth called out to Laurent.

"I'm in here," he answered.

She followed his voice to a small study at the end of the hall, where she found him working at a computer. The walls were lined with shelves of books, and the floor was covered with a braided wool rug. There was a comfortable-looking couch in a corner of the room that seemed perfect for curling up with a book.

A photograph of a woman hung on the wall near the door. The woman's smile, her eyes, and the shape of her chin were identical to Laurent's. Elizabeth assumed it was his mother, the late

Princess Marianne, who'd died when Laurent was ten years old.

On the other side of the room, in front of the window, an oak desk was piled high with papers and envelopes. "My goodness! Is all that your mail?" Elizabeth asked in amazement.

"Yes, it is," Laurent answered without looking up.

Elizabeth flinched at the dismissive tone in his voice. "You seem really busy."

"I am," he said.

Elizabeth shifted uneasily. She glanced down at the tray, suddenly feeling very foolish. "I thought you'd like some coffee, but . . ."

"Yes, thank you. Just set it down anywhere," he told her, obviously preoccupied.

Elizabeth set the tray on the desk next to the pile of mail, then took her own cup over to the couch. "I didn't know princes got so much mail," she remarked, trying to sound cheerful.

Laurent murmured something incoherent in response.

Elizabeth pressed her bottom lip between her teeth and slowly ran her finger around the rip of her cup. Apparently she'd picked a *terrible* time to drop in on him. "Laurent, I can see you're busy," she said. "Maybe I should come back later? I'll be free this evening after the children go to bed," she added hopefully.

Laurent turned to her, his expression masked. "No, I can finish this later." He stood up and stretched his arms over his head, then helped himself to the coffee she'd brought for him.

"I don't think it tastes as good as yours," Elizabeth said as she watched Laurent raise the cup to his lips.

"It's fine." He sat down on the couch with Elizabeth, leaving several feet between them. "How have you been?" he asked blandly.

Elizabeth put on a bright smile. "It's been very hectic at the château. Everyone is in a frenzy about the upcoming ball this weekend—even the children."

A sharp look flickered in his eyes. "Yes . . . the ball. It's very important to my family."

"I know," Elizabeth replied. "I'm a little nervous about it. All the fancy preparations and royal protocol . . . it seems overwhelming." She lowered her eyes and stared absently at the gold pattern on her cup. "I have this terrible fear that I'll embarrass myself among those noble types."

Elizabeth turned to Laurent, looking for reassurance.

"I can see how you would feel that way, not having been brought up in the culture," he said.

That wasn't what Elizabeth had wanted to hear him say. "Like you?" she asked, feeling stung.

"Like me." Laurent glanced at her, then stared out the window. "I'm a product of heritage, Elizabeth. We all are."

"But people are people, right?" Elizabeth countered, her voice tight and high-pitched. "How

92

much difference can there be between your people and mine?"

"An entire world," Laurent replied.

Elizabeth's heart sank. *What happened to the sweet, romantic guy who used to make me feel like a princess?* she sadly wondered. A long, tense silence filled the small room like a suffocating cloud. Elizabeth swallowed against the thickening lump in her throat. *Something is definitely wrong here,* she admitted to herself. She couldn't fool herself into believing that Laurent was simply preoccupied. The close bond they'd shared had been broken. A gulf of cold distance now stood between them, and Elizabeth didn't know how to reach him.

She exhaled a shaky breath. Her eyes stung, and she felt as though she might start sobbing any second. "My shift with the children starts in a few minutes, so I'd better get going," Elizabeth lied, rising to her feet and setting her empty cup back on the tray.

Laurent started to follow her, but she waved him back. "I can see myself out," she told him. He walked her to the front door anyway.

Elizabeth picked up the umbrella she'd left on a side table in the sitting room. "Thanks for the coffee," she said over her shoulder.

"Thank *you*, Elizabeth," he replied softly.

That sounds like a final good-bye, Elizabeth realized, hot tears streaming from her eyes as she rushed out of the cottage and into the pouring rain. *What did I do wrong?*

"This is so wonderful," Jessica whispered into Jacques's ear as they snuggled together on the beach Wednesday night. They had discovered the secluded spot tucked behind a ridge of high boulders earlier that evening and had immediately claimed it for themselves.

Now, as a silvery crescent moon shone like a jewel in the dark sky, Jessica and Jacques shared the chocolate-covered strawberries and sparkling cider he'd brought for her. Jessica felt as though she were being hypnotized by the crashing of the waves on the shore—and by the sexy glimmer in Jacques's brown eyes.

"Yes, wonderful," Jacques replied, punctuating his sentence with a gentle kiss.

Jessica felt a glorious sensation of pure happiness flowing through her heart. And although she and Jacques were a safe distance away from the château—and well hidden—the risk of being caught with the de Sainte-Maries' archenemy added to the excitement and romance.

"Tell me about Norveaux," Jessica said dreamily. "Is it beautiful?"

Jacques brushed his lips across her chin. "When I'm with you, *mon ange*, it is as if Norveaux doesn't exist."

Jessica's eyes narrowed. His words reminded

her of what the de Sainte-Maries' housekeeper had said about there being no Norveaux. "What do you mean?" she asked warily.

"No other world exists when I'm with you, Jessica. You are like everything to me. *Je t'aime de tout mon cœur.*"

"Oh," Jessica said with a laugh, pushing away her troublesome doubts. "And before we turn this into another French quiz—I also 'love you with all my heart.'"

Jacques flashed her a sexy grin. *"Tu es si belle."*

"You are so beautiful," Jessica translated, pleased with herself.

"Very good, mademoiselle," Jacques said. He picked up a fat strawberry and took a bite, then raised it to Jessica's lips. Giggling, she closed her teeth around it and took it from his fingers.

Jacques brushed a lock of her hair back from her face. "You are so special. . . ." He kissed her passionately.

Jessica shivered with delight as a million wonderful sensations danced up and down her spine.

Jacques abruptly ended the kiss. "But you are trembling?"

Jessica shot him a saucy grin. "I know."

"You're cold," he said.

"No, I'm not," she argued.

Jacques began rubbing his arms. "But I am. And the night air, it gives a chill. Let's go to the château, where it is warm."

Jessica leaned back and glared at him. "What about the feud? Aren't you concerned about being seen by the de Sainte-Maries?"

Jacques gave her a wicked, sexy grin. "We shall hide in your room."

Jessica laughed at his bold arrogance. "And what if I don't feel like inviting you up to my room?" she asked pointedly.

"I will beg, perhaps?" he replied sheepishly.

Jessica rolled her eyes. "Sometimes, Jacques . . . ," she said, her voice trailing off as she shook her head. "Are all French guys so strange?"

"Strange?" Jacques clutched his chest as if the word had stabbed his heart.

Jessica giggled. "How else could I describe a guy who'd rather be cooped up in a tiny room in the servants' quarters rather than lie here on this glorious beach?" She scooped up a handful of sand and let it sift through her fingers.

Jacques turned away and cleared his throat. "I must confess. You see, I feel . . . ill."

Jessica raised her eyebrows. "What?"

"I'm afraid the . . ." He raised his fist to his mouth and began coughing.

"What's wrong?" Jessica asked, suddenly concerned.

Jacques drew in a gasping breath and exhaled loudly. "I'm afraid the scratchy feeling I had in my throat this morning has become worse. And my head, it is pounding. If only I could rest for a few moments inside . . ."

Jessica eyed him suspiciously. She wasn't sure she believed him. After all, he'd seemed perfectly healthy a minute ago. But even if he were telling the truth, Jessica didn't want to risk being caught with him in the château—especially after her run-in with the countess the other night.

Jacques reached for her hand. "Come, Jessica. Let's go to your room." He started to get up, but she pulled him back down.

"I don't know if that's such a good idea," Jessica said. "There's a nasty witch and her spawn staying at the château for the summer. I met her in the hall late one night as I was going up to my room, and she freaked out. She accused me of abusing the Sainte-Maries' hospitality by running wild and dragging myself home at all hours. The scene got very ugly." Jessica sniffed indignantly. "I was afraid she'd pull out her evil wand and turn me into a toad."

Jacques tipped back his head and laughed. "I can't imagine you being afraid of anything," he remarked.

Jessica shrugged. "I'm usually not. But I'd hate to be sent back to Sweet Valley at this point. I'm sure they would if they caught me sneaking you up to my room."

"It is not so fair for you to be treated that way," Jacques said.

Jessica raised her knees to her chin and wrapped her arms around her legs. "I know," she replied. She gazed out at the darkened sea and exhaled a deep sigh. *This is going to be a legend someday,* she thought. *The romantic tale of the beautiful young maiden from Sweet Valley, California, who became the duchess of Norveaux after she'd captured the heart of a handsome—*

"You shouldn't let anyone push you around, *mon ange,*" Jacques said, interrupting her fantasy.

Jessica lifted an eyebrow. "Not even you?" she asked.

"Not even me," Jacques echoed softly.

Elizabeth pushed open the heavy iron gate at the entrance of the enclosed garden. She needed a quiet place to think, to sort out her confused feelings. Ever since she'd left Laurent's cottage the day before, she'd been trying to make sense of his sudden coldness.

Elizabeth moved slowly along the grassy path through the dense bushes and vines. She could barely distinguish between the foliage and shadows, but the darkness felt comforting and safe.

She passed the white stone shed that hid the entrance to the secret tunnels. Memories rushed through her mind as she recalled the night Laurent had brought her there after their moonlight picnic on the beach. "I *know* he cared for me," she whispered.

Elizabeth was surprised when she came to a wide clearing in the middle of the garden. Dark, leafy vines cascaded over the marble ledge that bordered the perimeter. A flowering tree grew in the center, its branches thickly covered with pale blossoms. Fallen petals were scattered around the base of the trunk like a circle of lace.

Elizabeth walked over to the iron bench on the other side of the clearing and sat down wearily. The children had been particularly trying that evening. She'd had to read the story about the bluebird prince six times to calm them down. Elizabeth had been tempted to rip the book to shreds by the time Princess Catherine had come in to tuck the children into their beds.

"I'm sick of fairy tales!" Elizabeth hissed. Her fantasies of living happily ever after with a handsome prince seemed utterly ridiculous. She must have been carried away by the splendor of the Château d'Amour Inconnu. Elizabeth vowed never to make that mistake again. *From now on I'll stick to reality,* she swore.

Elizabeth draped her arm along the back of the bench and absently traced a swirl in the wrought iron design. *But what Laurent and I had together was real,* her mind argued.

Elizabeth thought back to the time they'd spent riding through the forest, the things they'd said to each other . . . the flutter in her heart just before his lips would touch hers. . . .

A feeling of sadness welled up in Elizabeth's throat. Tears streamed down her cheeks.

Planting her feet on the bench, she wrapped her arms around her legs and rested her forehead on her raised knees. "What happened?" she asked herself, sobbing. First Todd had broken her heart and now Laurent. *Is there something wrong with me?* she wondered.

Antonia's cruel, taunting words echoed in her mind: *"It's when you're standing next to nobility that you look your shabbiest."* Elizabeth shook her head, firmly dismissing the ridiculous insult from her mind. Just because she wasn't born into nobility didn't make her inferior. A person would have to be very narrow-minded and backward to hold such an old-fashioned attitude. *Laurent isn't like that*, she thought.

But a strong feeling of doubt hovered in her mind like a dark, heavy storm cloud. *Did Laurent decide to end our relationship because I'm not high-class enough for him and his royal family?* she wondered.

Elizabeth drew in a shaky breath and swiped her hand across her damp cheeks. If Laurent wasn't interested in her because she was a commoner, then it was his problem—not hers. She was proud to be an American, where everybody was considered equal. And she was also extremely proud to be a *Wakefield.* Her parents worked hard to provide for her, Jessica, and Steven, and that meant more to Elizabeth than all the vast holdings and power of the de Sainte-Marie family.

A sudden scraping noise startled her. Elizabeth whirled around and saw Laurent walking along the marble ledge toward her. Her whole body stiffened, all of her senses on alert.

"Elizabeth . . . ," he whispered. "I've been searching for you everywhere."

She cast him a scathing look and turned away.

"May I sit down?" he asked.

Elizabeth squeezed her eyes shut and rested her forehead on her knees again. *Leave me alone!* she silently pleaded. Her heart had suffered enough.

After a few seconds she felt his hand on her back. "Please, Elizabeth. Look at me."

She raised her head and glared at him. "What do you want?" she snapped.

Laurent sat down beside her and leaned forward, bracing his elbows on his knees. "I suppose I deserve that."

A sensation of cold anger shivered through her, numbing her pain. "I don't know what you think you deserve, *Prince* Laurent . . . and I don't care. If you're too proud to associate with an American, that's your loss!"

Laurent bolted upright and turned to her with a wide-eyed, astonished look on his face. "But you are wrong about me!"

"Am I?" Elizabeth asked bitingly. "Ever since I arrived at Château d'Amour Inconnu, I've been treated like an inferior being because my family doesn't have a pedigree."

Laurent reeled back as if she'd slapped him. "I

101

never treated you like that," he whispered. "To me, you're perfect as you are."

Elizabeth clenched her jaw, steeling her heart against him. "Those are nice words," she retorted. "But I'm not a fool, Laurent. I know when I'm being pushed out of someone's life."

"No, it is not that way!" Laurent shook his head. "I never meant to give you such an impression."

"What about yesterday at the cottage?" Elizabeth swallowed against the thickening lump in her throat. "You totally ignored me, as if I were an unwelcome pest."

Laurent uttered a sorrowful groan. "Never! You are always welcome to me," he said. He shifted so that he was facing her and draped his arm along the back of the bench. "I'm sorry for the way I acted. It is why this evening I had to see you—to apologize."

Elizabeth felt her anger beginning to thaw, but the hurt and confusion were still there. "I need an explanation," she told him. "I want to understand what was going on between us yesterday."

Laurent's gaze moved over her face, as if he were memorizing her. "I was so happy to see you, Elizabeth," he said at last. "But there was something on my mind. I've been troubled lately . . . things I have to work out for myself." He paused. "Can you forgive me?" he asked.

Elizabeth lowered her eyes. "I want to believe you, Laurent. But—"

Laurent curved his arm around her shoulders and gently pulled her toward him. "Be patient with me," he pleaded.

Elizabeth felt the protective wall she'd built around her heart tumbling down. She couldn't ignore the love that shone from the depths of Laurent's blue eyes. "I do forgive you," she breathed.

Laurent smiled tenderly. Then he kissed her, melting her heart completely.

Elizabeth felt tears of happiness spring into her eyes. "This is like a dream," she whispered.

Laurent held her close. "This isn't a dream, Elizabeth. I love you forever." She could feel his heart pounding as rapidly as her own.

"I love you too," she whispered.

Laurent kissed her again, and Elizabeth allowed herself to be swept up in the passion. She became aware of the beauty of the night, the bright crescent moon that shone in the black sky, the sweet lavender fragrance on the night breezes, and the glorious sensation of being in Laurent's arms again.

"I can't believe I let you talk me into this," Jessica complained to Jacques as they crept up the stone staircase to her room. "If we get caught, I'll be on the next plane back to Sweet Valley for sure!"

When they reached her door, Jacques pulled her close and touched his lips to hers. Jessica swayed against him and laced her fingers behind his neck.

Suddenly a burst of female chatter on the stairs brought Jessica back to her senses. Snapping to attention, she grabbed Jacques by the sleeve of his shirt and dragged him into her room. Peeking from behind the door, Jessica watched as two maids appeared on the landing.

She pushed the door closed all the way and leaned back against it. "That was close," she breathed.

Jacques was stretched out on her bed, his arms tucked under her pillow. He raised his head slightly and groaned.

Jessica crossed her arms and eyed him narrowly. *He seemed fine all the way up here,* she realized. "Jacques, what's going on?" she asked. "You're not really sick, are you?"

He began coughing violently. "Water," he gasped.

Jessica rolled her eyes. But she decided to play along just in case he wasn't faking. "I'll be back in a minute," she told him. "Stay in here."

Still coughing, Jacques nodded. Jessica opened the door slightly and checked to see if anyone was coming.

"All clear," she whispered to Jacques over her shoulder.

He sucked in a gasping breath, clutching his throat, and nodded again. But the instant she stepped out into the hall, the sound of his coughing abruptly stopped.

Jessica's brow furrowed and she pursed her lips. *A miraculous recovery?* she thought doubtfully. Now she was more than suspicious—she was absolutely certain he was up to something.

Jessica felt a surge of annoyance. Obviously he'd staged the whole sickness routine and desperate plea for water so that he could be alone in her room. *To do what?* she wondered. Determined to find out, she inched open the door and spied on Jacques through the crack.

He was sitting hunched over on the edge of the bed, his elbows resting on his knees. His gaze was fixed on something he held in his hands. At first Jessica thought he was reading. Bemused, she opened the door a little wider to get a better look.

Jessica's jaw dropped as she recognized the object in his hands. It was the red jewelry case she kept under her pillow. For a moment she was too stunned to move or to utter a sound. *Who does he think he is, going through my personal things?* she fumed silently.

She saw him slip the case into his pocket, and her blood began to boil. *He* knows *how much that pendant means to me!* she thought.

Jessica stiffened her spine, pulled back her shoulders, and took a deep breath. Primed for battle, she burst into the room.

Royal duke or not, Jacques Landeau needed to learn a few things about respect.

Chapter 7

Jessica lunged at Jacques, toppling him sideways on the bed before he had a chance to react. With a swift movement she grabbed the jewelry case out of his shirt pocket and whipped it behind her back. "This is mine!" she hissed in his face.

Jacques recovered instantly and sprang toward her. His arms shot out, capturing her in a tight embrace as he reached behind her. Giggling hysterically, Jessica struggled against him, twisting and buckling to loosen his hold. She managed to roll onto her back, her hands and the jewelry case tucked safely underneath her.

Jacques leaned over her, his face looming inches above hers, his lips curled in a challenging grin. A thrilling combination of fear and excitement shivered up and down Jessica's spine.

"You are a very stubborn girl," he whispered.

"Me?" Jessica replied breathlessly. "What about *you?*" Suddenly she felt his hand slip under her back, groping for the case.

Jessica shrieked. Digging her heels into the mattress, she scrambled away from him. Jacques made a grab for her, but Jessica jerked out of his grasp. Laughing excitedly, she rolled off the bed and scurried halfway across the room.

The air crackled with electricity as she and Jacques glared at each other, their eyes locked in a heated battle of wills.

Finally Jacques uttered an exasperated sound and shook his head. "Jessica, sometimes this *vigueur* you have . . . it is like the *énergie atomique.*"

Jessica flashed him a saucy grin. "*Atomic energy*—I like that," she replied. "But flattery isn't going to save you now, Your *Royalness.* If I don't hear an extremely sincere apology from you in the next five seconds, I'll blow up like an atomic *bomb!*"

Laughing, Jacques raised his hands in surrender. "I wanted to make a surprise for you. That is why I pretended an illness."

Jessica snorted. "You should take acting lessons. I wasn't fooled at all."

Jacques clutched his heart and twisted his face into an exaggerated mask of pain. Jessica pressed her lips together to keep from laughing. She refused to let down her guard until things between her and Jacques were resolved—to *her* satisfaction.

Jacques dropped the silly charade and eyed

Jessica with a deep, soulful look. "Come here," he said softly, beckoning to her with his arms.

Jessica remained seated on the floor. "I can hear your apology just fine from right here," she told him.

Jacques threw up his hands and muttered some French words under his breath. "But it is *your* surprise to find," he insisted, gesturing toward the pillow on her bed.

Jessica's eyes narrowed, her curiosity piqued. "You brought me a present?" she asked, rising to her feet.

"Oui." Jacques lifted a corner of the pillow and picked up a small package wrapped in newspaper. "Voilà," he said, holding it out toward Jessica. "But to surprise you is most difficult," he added dryly.

Jessica grinned, beaming with delight as she accepted the gift. She tucked her red jewelry case under her pillow, then sat down beside Jacques and began unwrapping her new gift.

"It's beautiful!" Jessica exclaimed as she lifted the delicate pearl bracelet from its nest of old newspaper. The pearls were sewn in flower patterns, with seed pearl clusters surrounding a larger, center pearl, creating little flowers that were strung at regular intervals between gold and pearl links. Jessica draped it over her wrist, admiring the way the snowy white pearls contrasted against her tanned skin.

"You like it?" Jacques asked.

Jessica turned to him and smiled. "I *love* it," she

replied. She leaned over and kissed him. "Thank you, Jacques."

"The pearls are genuine," he said as he fastened the gold clasp for her. "Now I can take back that ghastly fake stone I gave you on the train."

Jessica sprang forward and grabbed the case from under the pillow. "I *told* you, I don't care if it's a fake," she said, holding it away from him. "This pendant is very special to me."

"But Jessica, *mon ange* . . . ," he pleaded. "I only gave it to you because I had nothing better at the time. It is . . . *junk*. The bracelet is for you."

Jessica glanced down at her wrist. "And I'll treasure it forever," she vowed. "But the pendant means a lot to me."

Jacques pushed his hand through his hair. "Jessica, remember on the train . . . when I gave you that stone. I promised I would replace it someday. And now I have."

Jessica tightened her hold around the case. "What are you going to do with it?" Then a suspicious thought popped into her head, responding to her own question. "Are you going to keep it handy in case another pretty girl happens to come along?" she asked bitingly.

Jacques shook his head, laughing. "When I first saw you, I—" He abruptly fell silent as footsteps sounded on the stairs.

Jacques and Jessica exchanged alarmed looks, their skirmish overshadowed by the present emergency.

Jessica glanced toward the door and noticed that she'd left it wide open. Cursing under her breath, she rushed over and shut it firmly.

Her heart beating furiously, Jessica pressed her ear against the door to listen. She held her breath as the footsteps came closer . . . and stopped. Then someone knocked on the door. Jessica jumped, her heart in her throat.

"Jessica, are you in there?" Anna's voice called through the door.

Now what? Jessica wondered, her body gripped with panic. She glanced at Jacques over her shoulder.

His face was pale, his deep brown eyes wide and luminous. "Answer her," he mouthed.

Jessica nodded. She tried to speak, but only a strange gasping sound came out. Jessica swallowed, drew in a strangled breath, and tried again. "Yes, Anna?"

"May I come in?" Anna asked.

"Um . . . just a minute," Jessica muttered, her whole body trembling.

Jacques gave her a reassuring wink and crept under the bed. Jessica noticed her blue silk robe on the floor in front of her bureau. With a sudden flash of inspiration she grabbed it and hastily slipped it on over her clothes.

Jessica inched open the door. Anna was standing in the hall, her eyes lowered to the clipboard in her hands.

"Um . . . A-Anna . . . ," Jessica stammered.

Anna looked up and smiled briskly. "We have details to talk over for the ball that concern the children."

Jessica clutched the front edges of her robe at her throat. "I was just getting ready for bed," she lied.

Anna nodded. "It's good I arrive now, before you are asleep." Suddenly someone hollered to the housekeeper from the staircase. Anna exhaled sharply and grumbled in French. "I'll be just a moment, Jessica," she said. "The ball this weekend makes everything in a chaos."

Thank you, lucky stars! Jessica thought as she quickly shut the door. She slumped back against it and exhaled a sigh of relief. Jacques squirmed out of his hiding place.

"That was way too close," Jessica said to him.

Jacques sat down on the bed and buried his face in his hands. "This is a disaster. Never I wished to cause you such trouble, *mon ange.*" She could see how concerned he was for her, and it warmed her heart.

Jessica smiled tenderly and went over to sit beside him. "It's not *that* big a deal," she said, slipping her arms around his waist. "No one ever came out and directly said that I'm not allowed to have a guy in my room."

Jacques raised his head and gave her a small, grateful smile. "But if they see *me* . . ."

"So what?" Jessica countered. "This feud between your families is totally ridiculous. And anyway, it probably won't last much longer. I'm sure things will improve drastically when you and Laurent are in charge." *And when I'm the duchess of Norveaux and my very own twin sister is the princess de Sainte-Marie,* Jessica added silently.

Jacques framed her face with his hands and gently stroked her chin with his thumb. "Sometimes I feel the things in my life will never improve," he said in a soft, faraway voice. "I wanted so much more for you . . . for *us.*"

Jessica's heart melted. "This is more than enough for now," she said. She flashed him a wide, flirty smile. "I think it's *incredibly* romantic to sneak around with you."

Jacques curved his hand around the back of her neck, sending tingles up and down her spine. She closed her eyes as his lips touched hers. Jacques kissed her gently at first, then deeper, until Jessica felt as if she were drowning in a sweet, warm pool of honey.

Enveloped in such luscious, swirling sensations, she almost missed the slight tug on her hand. In a heartbeat a warning flashed through her mind. Still locked in the kiss, Jessica snapped to attention. She realized Jacques had one arm behind her back and was trying to pry the jewelry case out of her hand.

This guy doesn't know when to give up! she thought. Giggling against his lips, she swung her hand behind her own back. Jacques started laughing too. They kept the kiss going as another playful tug-of-war for the pendant broke out between them.

Suddenly a door slammed somewhere nearby and female chatter erupted in the hallway. Jessica and Jacques broke apart and froze.

"We must be crazy!" Jessica muttered. "Anna will be back any minute. You have to get out of here!"

Jacques nodded and slowly dragged himself up to his feet.

"Hurry!" Jessica urged.

Jacques walked over to the door, opened it a crack, and peered out. Then he looked back over his shoulder and blew Jessica a kiss. "I love you," he whispered.

Jessica gave him a dazzling smile. *"Je t'aime,"* she echoed in French.

Jacques crept down the stairs, his fists clenched in frustration. Once again he'd failed miserably. Jacques thought the pearl bracelet he'd lifted from Carlotta when he'd gone sailing with her, Monica, and his father a few days ago would do the trick. Carlotta had carelessly tossed it on a deck chair when she'd taken a swim and had forgotten all about it by the time she'd dried off.

But Jacques hadn't realized how attached Jessica had grown to the emerald. *Her heart is sentimental,* he reminded himself. It was one of the things he loved about her—but it was causing him such trouble.

His father's warning about their client came back to him, stopping him cold. *He's not the kind of man to whom one brings bad news,* Louis had warned. Jacques knew exactly what his father had meant. He'd grown up with people who lusted after treasures and who would do *anything* to satisfy their desires. They weren't very forgiving when they didn't get what they'd been promised.

An icy shiver of fear sliced through Jacques's gut. The stakes were too high for him to quit now. He couldn't return to his father empty-handed.

Elizabeth felt as though she were gliding on a dreamy cloud when she returned to the château that evening. Although she was realistic enough to know that she and Laurent had many things to work out, Elizabeth clung to the fact that they loved each other deeply. They would have to deal with the future one step at a time.

As she walked toward the stairs she heard voices coming from the kitchen. Preparations for the weekend ball had been going on night and day, so Elizabeth wasn't surprised. She was just about to poke her head in the open doorway and wave good night when suddenly she heard her name mentioned.

Elizabeth stopped in her tracks and pressed her back against the wall next to the door. She recognized Brigitte's voice, speaking rapidly in French. Elizabeth was able to figure out only some of what the maid was saying.

"Suddenly he appeared . . . his face aglow . . .

his eyes only for her . . . ," Brigitte said.

Elizabeth's eyes widened. She realized Brigitte was talking about the morning Laurent had surprised her and the children in the nursery. Then she heard Henri the gardener's deep, melodic voice recounting the evening he'd seen her and Laurent riding away on horseback.

Elizabeth's cheeks burned with indignation. *They're gossiping about us!* she fumed. Suddenly she heard the word *"fiançailles,"* and an alarm went off in her head. "A *betrothal?*" she translated under her breath.

A female voice Elizabeth didn't recognize chimed into the conversation. The woman spoke with a slightly different accent than the others. "I'm certain the engagement will be announced this weekend. Though I never thought the prince would go through with it."

Elizabeth pressed her fingers against her lips as she continued to eavesdrop.

"The marriage will benefit the royal family," a different maid remarked.

"But what about Elizabeth?" Brigitte asked.

"In time . . . ," Henri began in a low, pensive voice, "the American girl will realize the ways of the nobility and find her happiness."

Elizabeth's jaw dropped, her heart in her throat. She was totally stunned and a bit horrified. *Laurent is planning to* marry *me?* she thought. *They'll announce our engagement this weekend . . .*

and I'm just supposed to adjust *to everything?*
She'd assumed that she and Laurent would be able
to take their relationship one step at a time, but
apparently she'd been wrong.

Elizabeth darted past the doorway and raced
up to her room. She headed straight for her antique desk, plunked herself down in the chair, and
whipped open her journal. Her hand shook as she
picked up her pen.

Writing usually helped her make sense of things,
and at that moment Elizabeth needed it more than
ever. She was desperate to impose order on her
dizzying confusion. Thoughts and emotions were
thrashing through her mind, totally out of control.

Jessica lay sprawled across her bed, her head
bursting with romantic dreams as she gazed at her
bracelet. She imagined herself and Jacques, standing in the balcony of a glorious palace, waving to
the cheering crowds below. Jessica sighed. *I'll bet
Norveaux is the most awesome place in the world,*
she thought.

She rubbed her fingertip over one of the pearls.
The surface felt warm and smooth. Jessica decided
it was the most beautiful bracelet she'd ever seen.
Maybe when Elizabeth saw it, she'd finally realize
what a sweet, considerate guy Jacques really was.

Jessica grinned slyly. She'd heard her twin return and go into her room a short time earlier.
There's no time like the present, she reasoned.

She padded across the hall barefooted and knocked on her sister's door. Not bothering to wait for an answer, Jessica breezed into the room.

Elizabeth was sitting at her desk, writing furiously. "Do you mind, Jess?" she grumbled without looking up.

Jessica plopped down on the bed, undaunted by her twin's response. Elizabeth was always cranky at first when anyone disturbed her writing. "Notice anything different about me?" Jessica asked with an exaggerated, teasing drawl.

Elizabeth snapped her diary shut and twisted around in the chair. "Can't you see I'm busy?"

Jessica giggled and draped her arm gracefully over the side of the bed. "I think my wrist looks especially awesome this evening, don't you?"

Elizabeth sighed wearily. "I give up. What's on your mind?"

Jessica snorted. "Not my mind, silly." She stretched her arm out in front of her, the circle of pearls gleaming on her wrist. "Jacques gave it to me this evening," she said proudly.

Elizabeth barely glanced at it. "It's nice," she said flatly.

Jessica bolted upright and glared at her sister. "*Nice* is when a guy gives you flowers or a CD. This bracelet is totally awesome."

Elizabeth gave her a contrite smile. "I'm just a bit preoccupied tonight," she said, pushing back the chair. She came over and sat down beside Jessica.

Jessica held up the bracelet, allowing her twin to admire it properly. "What do you think?" she asked, fishing for praise.

Elizabeth nodded. "It's breathtaking, Jess."

"That's much better," Jessica replied with a laugh. She lowered her arm and sighed dreamily. "I've decided that Lila was right all along—France is the most romantic place in the world."

All of a sudden, without any warning, Elizabeth burst into tears.

Jessica gasped a quick, startled breath. "What's wrong?" she asked, putting her arms around her twin.

"Laurent," Elizabeth sobbed.

Jessica felt her heart sink. She assumed Elizabeth was crying because she'd found out that Laurent was betrothed to Antonia. *I can't believe he'd prefer that sickly-looking snob over Liz!* Jessica thought hotly.

"I'm confused," Elizabeth wailed. "France is nice . . . but *forever?* Besides, I'm way too young to get"—she hiccuped loudly—"married."

Totally baffled by what she was hearing, Jessica leaned back and looked her sister in the eye. "What are you talking about?" she asked.

Elizabeth shook her head. "He's going to ask me to marry him."

Yes! Jessica mentally cheered. *Thank goodness I didn't tell Liz about Laurent and Antonia!*

"Everything is happening so fast." Elizabeth

sniffed noisily. "I need a tissue," she muttered, scooting off the bed.

Jessica's gaze followed her across the room. *If Elizabeth and Laurent get married, I'll have a bona fide prince for a brother-in-law,* she realized excitedly. Everything was turning out even better than Jessica had dared to hope.

Elizabeth took the tissue box from the desk and brought it back to the bed. "Laurent is a wonderful guy," she said pensively. "And what we have is very special. We like a lot of the same things, and we care about each other as friends."

"So what's the problem?" Jessica asked.

Elizabeth sighed. "I'm too young! And I'm not ready to get married. I mean, I love Laurent . . . at least I *think* I love him." She shrugged. "I really haven't known him that long. Maybe it's just that I *want* to be in love with him."

Jessica rolled her eyes. "Or maybe it's just that you think too much!"

Elizabeth cracked a smile. "You would say that."

"Because it's true!" Jessica insisted. "Now promise me you won't make any major decisions without talking to me first."

Elizabeth laughed at that. "That's just about the most ridiculous advice I've ever gotten. Anyway, as I was walking by the kitchen a few minutes ago, I overheard—"

She was interrupted by a knock on the door. "That's probably Anna," Jessica said, getting up to answer it. "She said she'd be back in one minute—ages ago." Jessica giggled to herself. *If I'd known how long one of Anna's minutes really was, I wouldn't have hurried Jacques out of my room so quickly.*

Jessica opened the door, and Anna breezed into the room, clutching her clipboard to her chest. "It is good you're both here," she said.

Elizabeth pulled the chair out from under her desk. "Please sit down, Anna," she offered politely.

Jessica smiled to herself. *When Liz becomes the princess around here, I hope these people realize how lucky they are to have her instead of Antonia,* she thought.

Anna glanced at Jessica. "You are no longer dressed with your, how you say . . . *par-jee-mas?*"

"You mean *pajamas?*" Elizabeth asked.

Jessica looked down at her black jeans and gulped, remembering her charade with the blue robe earlier.

"Pajamas," Anna repeated slowly. "I learn better my English with you, like the children."

"I changed," Jessica blurted. "I decided it was much too early to go to bed. I've been getting way too much sleep lately."

Elizabeth shot her a suspicious look, which Jessica ignored.

"Now, for the tableau," Anna began, glancing down at her clipboard. "It will be played before the ball on Saturday evening, and the princess leaves the children's part to you."

"Tableau?" Jessica questioned, looking to her twin for a translation.

Elizabeth's eyes narrowed. "Tableau? That means blackboard, doesn't it?"

Anna smiled. "That's one translation, yes. *Tableau* means also painting or scene. For the game each team chooses a scene from a story, then conveys it on the stage by posing as the characters," she explained.

"Sort of like charades?" Elizabeth asked.

Anna nodded. "But in tableau you must remain totally still for five minutes. Everyone dresses with the fancy costumes, and then the group freezes into a paintinglike scene. The audience must guess what story the scene is from. It is much fun."

Elizabeth chuckled. "Sounds interesting, but I don't know how we're going to get the kids to go along with it. It'll be torture for them to keep still for longer than two seconds."

"They'll love it," Jessica countered. "We'll find ourselves some fantastic costumes to wear. . . ." She pictured herself decked out in a fabulous gown, looking breathtakingly awesome. She'd finally have a chance to show that old countess a taste of real glamour.

Jessica caught herself staring at her pearl bracelet. *Too bad Jacques won't be there to see me,* she thought sadly.

Chapter 8

Sitting beside Jacques in the elegant throne room of their huge castle in Norveaux, Jessica opened the sealed message one of the butlers had just handed her on a gold tray. She smiled as she read the note. "My dearest friend from Sweet Valley, Lila Fowler, has just arrived for a visit," Jessica told her husband, the duke. She turned to the team of servants in fancy dress uniform who stood at attention beside her throne, waiting to jump at her slightest command. "Please show Miss Fowler in," Jessica requested in a cultured, regal tone of voice.

"As you wish, Your Highness," they answered, bowing respectfully.

A moment later the huge double doors were opened, and there was Lila, her eyes popping in awe and her complexion turning green with envy. . . .

Suddenly a loud, angry screech outside her

bedroom knocked Jessica right out of her glorious dream. She awoke with a start, a corner of the sheet clenched in her fist. *How is a person supposed to get any sleep around here?* she fumed. Doors were slamming up and down the hall, heavy footsteps pounding on the stairs. Voices were shouting in rapid-fire French.

Knowing she wouldn't be able to go back to her dream, Jessica threw off the bedcovers and swung her legs over the edge of the mattress. "This better be an emergency," she grumbled as she pushed her fists into the sleeves of her robe. She stepped into the hall and was nearly knocked to the floor by a rushing stampede of bodies.

Flattened against the wall, Jessica gaped at the strange scene. Servants ran around hysterically. The countess stormed through the hall in a bright blue filmy chiffon robe, with a white turban wrapped around her head, screaming, *"Au secours! Au secours!"* Antonia, wearing green silk pajamas, trailed her mother, clutching a shawl around her shoulders and sobbing hysterically.

Jessica covered her mouth and smirked discreetly. She presumed the di Riminis were hysterical over Laurent's having chosen Elizabeth over Antonia. *Seems those hags are extremely poor losers!* she thought snidely.

Then Anna made her way through the crowd, her face pale and her expression grave. Princess Catherine was right behind her. Jessica began to suspect that something worse than Antonia's broken engagement had happened. But even though her French had improved since she'd arrived at the château, she couldn't understand much of what was being shouted.

Jessica saw Elizabeth standing in the doorway of her room, watching the commotion with a look of astonishment. "What's going on?" Jessica mouthed.

Elizabeth inched her way over to Jessica. "I don't know exactly. Something terrible, I think."

"What's that the witch keeps yelling?" Jessica asked. "*Oh* something or other?"

"*Au secours*," Elizabeth said. "It means *help*."

Jessica waved over a maid who was standing near the stairs. "Do you know what this is all about?" she asked.

The girl stepped closer to the twins and shook her head, babbling something incoherent. "She doesn't speak English," Elizabeth explained. She began talking to the maid in French.

"What is she saying?" Jessica demanded impatiently, nudging her twin's shoulder. Elizabeth shrugged Jessica's hand away.

"Antonia's diamond necklace is missing," Elizabeth said at last.

Jessica sniggered. "Serves them right."

"The countess insists that one of the servants must've stolen it," Elizabeth added.

"That's ridiculous!" Jessica spat. "Antonia is such a ditz, she probably misplaced it."

Suddenly the countess's eyes locked on Jessica's, and her mouth twisted with rage. "Them!" she bellowed in English as she came over to the twins.

Jessica winced and touched her hand to her ear. The woman could probably outyell the entire Sweet Valley High cheerleading squad.

The countess glared at them, her massive chest heaving. The loose flesh around her jaw flapped and jiggled. "I demand these two be strip-searched at once!"

Jessica heard Elizabeth gasp, and a sudden, hot flame of defiant anger flared in her gut. *Who does that ugly hag think she is, trying to intimidate us like that!* she raged inwardly.

Jessica raised her head high, her fists clenched at her sides. She was sick of being treated like a lowly, scum-of-the-earth peon, but to see her sister being treated as one was more than she could stand. She met the witch's glare straight on. "I'd like to see you *try*," Jessica retorted.

The woman sputtered indignantly, obviously shocked that anyone would dare stand up to her. *Get used to it, Your Evilness,* Jessica thought, relishing the small victory.

Princess Catherine came up behind the countess, her complexion starkly pale. She patted the angry woman's shoulders and spoke to her in French in a soothing tone of voice. Jessica guessed the princess was telling the old witch to calm down.

Princess Catherine glanced at Jessica and

Elizabeth. "It is all a simple mistake, I am certain," she added with a thick French accent.

Jessica assumed the princess had switched to English for her and Elizabeth's benefit, and she was touched by the gesture. *She obviously doesn't believe the countess's ravings either,* Jessica thought.

"A simple mistake?" the countess raged. "A thief crept into my daughter's room in the middle of the night and stole the diamond necklace that had been her grandmother's." She threw her arms around Antonia and began sobbing hysterically. "What if my poor little girl had been murdered in her sleep?"

"The world would be a better place," Jessica muttered sarcastically under her breath. She didn't think she'd spoken loud enough to be heard . . . until she felt Elizabeth pinch her elbow.

"Ouch!" Jessica hissed, rubbing the painful spot and trying not to laugh.

Prince Nicolas appeared at the top of the stairs, and everyone fell silent. "The guards have been notified and the police are on their way," he announced.

"Those girls are the culprits, I am certain!" the countess insisted, pointing an accusing finger at Jessica and Elizabeth. "I want the police to arrest them."

"Let's go have some nice hot tea," Princess Catherine suggested, leading her hysterical guest toward the stairs. She gave the twins a quick smile over her shoulder, as if to reassure them that everything would be OK.

After they left, Anna clapped for attention and spoke sharply to everyone in French. "What is she saying?" Jessica asked Elizabeth.

"She's ordering everyone to go to work immediately," Elizabeth replied. "I suppose I should get ready to meet the kids for breakfast."

Jessica lifted her hand and gave a little wave. "My shift doesn't begin until noon. If all the fun is over for now, I'm going back to bed."

Elizabeth rolled her eyes. "Jessica, only *you* would consider a jewel theft and the threat of a strip search *fun*."

"No, the hands on the head!" Claudine hollered at Elizabeth, shaking her head vigorously. The children had wanted to teach Elizabeth the movements to one of their singing games, but her concentration skills that day were totally dismal. Pierre and Manon had already given up and were now rolling on the nursery floor, laughing at her.

Elizabeth put her hands on her hips and shot them all a playful snarl.

Suddenly the door opened and Jessica breezed into the nursery. "Hi, guys," she called cheerfully.

Elizabeth sagged melodramatically with relief. "I'm saved from further humiliation," she declared.

Jessica giggled. "I would have been earlier, but I heard the storm troopers coming down the hall, and I had to duck into the bathroom until they passed."

Elizabeth frowned, bemused. "Storm troopers?"

Jessica nodded. "The countess is marching the police through the château, screaming at them in French. Antonia is with them too, sobbing her eyes out," she added with a grin.

Elizabeth shuddered, remembering the countess's expression when she'd demanded that she and Jessica be strip-searched. "I just hope they find that necklace," she said.

"Isn't it cool?" Jessica asked excitedly.

Elizabeth blinked. "Cool?"

"Yeah!" Jessica exclaimed. She turned to the children. "Why don't you kids go play with your blocks," she suggested. "Let's see who can make the best tower."

The children squealed with delight and scampered off to get their blocks. Elizabeth laughed as she watched them go, then sent her twin a wry look. "Jess, explain to me again how we're going to get them to stay perfectly still for the tableau."

"They'll be fine," Jessica replied hastily as she led Elizabeth to the couch and sat her down. "Anyway, I've been thinking." She lowered her voice. "Maybe if we keep our eyes open, we'll be the ones to catch the jewel thief."

Elizabeth snorted. "Come on, this is real life. If the diamond necklace was stolen, the thief would be long gone by now. I think you've seen too many spy movies," she teased.

"But don't you think it's weird that there have

been two thefts since we've been on this trip?" Jessica persisted.

"It is kind of a strange coincidence," Elizabeth agreed. She thought about it for a moment, considering the possibilities. "Do you think the thief is someone here at the château?"

Jessica nodded. "I'm sure of it," she declared. "I have a pretty good idea who it is."

"Who?" Elizabeth asked.

"The countess!" Jessica replied emphatically.

Elizabeth rolled her eyes. "Jessica, just because she's a mean witch doesn't automatically mean she's a thief. Besides, why would she steal her own family heirloom and her daughter's diamond necklace?"

Jessica leaned closer, her eyes flashing excitedly. "Insurance!"

"Insurance for what?" Elizabeth questioned.

"The insurance *money*," Jessica clarified. "Rich people always take out huge insurance policies on their jewelry so that if they lose them, they can collect the money. Lila even suggested that we get insurance for the earrings Grandma sent us."

Elizabeth automatically fingered one of the diamond posts in her ear. "Insurance fraud is a major crime," she reflected. "Do you really think the countess is capable of something so serious?"

Jessica snorted. "Don't you?"

"I'm not sure," Elizabeth responded, her mind clicking. Her reporter instincts shifted into gear. "But I'd sure love to get to the bottom of this."

Later that day Elizabeth sat in her room, looking over her notes. She'd already filled seven pages of a yellow legal pad with her ideas and observations about the thefts. "Both items belonged to the di Riminis . . . one missing from the train . . . one from the château . . . ," she read. "The diamond necklace was stolen from Antonia's room in the château, and the di Riminis' family heirloom was stolen from the countess's luggage."

Elizabeth circled the word *heirloom* and drew a big question mark next to it. She didn't know what the heirloom object was exactly and made a mental note to find out.

Elizabeth realized that she and Jessica were the most obvious suspects. They were the only people who had been on the train *and* who were staying at the château.

Except for the countess and Antonia, of course, Elizabeth reflected. The more she considered the possibilities, the more convinced she was of the countess's guilt. All her bluster and rage in the servants' wing that morning might have been nothing more than an attempt to divert suspicion from herself.

Suddenly the door burst open and Jessica rushed in. "Come on, Liz, let's go!"

Elizabeth jumped up, responding to the urgency in her twin's voice. "Go where?" she asked, following Jessica to the stairs. "And where are the kids?"

"They're having their picture taken," Jessica

replied over her shoulders. "A hot-looking photographer is here to do a formal portrait of the royal family. The witches too, lucky for us. But I don't know how much time that gives us. . . ."

Elizabeth stopped her on the second-floor landing. "Time for what?" she demanded.

"To find the jewel," Jessica hissed.

Elizabeth's mouth snapped shut, and she shivered with excitement. *We just might crack this case*, she thought.

"I'm pretty sure the countess's suite is in the east wing," Jessica whispered when they reached the bottom floor. "I overheard some of the maids complaining about her constant demands for room service."

"Figures," Elizabeth said wryly.

A few minutes later they crept into the east wing. The hallway was softly illuminated by huge crystal chandeliers in the ceiling. Framed paintings and tapestries hung on the walls, and a plush red carpet runner covered the floor. Settees with red velvet cushions, marble-topped tables, and gleaming suits of armor stood at intervals between the closed doors along the length of the hall. Dozens of potted plants added a softening touch to the formal decor.

"I wish we were staying here," Jessica complained.

"Do you know which room is the countess's?" Elizabeth asked. Jessica shook her head.

Elizabeth tiptoed to the first door and pressed her ear against it. Holding her breath, she listened for any noise that might indicate someone was inside the room. But all she heard was the heavy pounding of her heart. Steeling her fluttering nerves, Elizabeth twisted the knob and slowly opened the door.

"This is the countess's room," Jessica whispered right behind her.

Elizabeth hesitated. "Are you sure?"

"Of course." Jessica waltzed into the huge sitting room and pointed to a filmy yellow chiffon gown with black feathery trim that was draped over the arm of an ornate antique couch. "I'd recognize those ostrich feathers anywhere," Jessica said.

Elizabeth chuckled nervously under her breath.

There were two bedrooms in the suite and three bathrooms. French doors in the sitting room and each bedroom opened up to a wide balcony overlooking the east gardens. "What a waste!" Jessica remarked as they made a brief investigation of the suite. "All this for those two . . . we should have had a suite like this!" Then she grinned. "But I suppose we'll be living in this kind of luxury soon enough, when you're the princess de Sainte-Marie and I'm the duchess of Norveaux."

Elizabeth flinched. She wasn't sure she wanted to be a French princess. *We have a job to do here,* she reminded herself firmly, dragging herself back to the reality of the moment. "Where would the countess have hidden her diamond necklace?" Elizabeth wondered aloud.

"It could be here anywhere," Jessica replied. She pushed up the sleeves of her sweater. "Let's get started."

They checked out the sitting room first, from top to bottom and corner to corner. Elizabeth crawled out onto the balcony on her hands and knees to avoid the possibility of being seen from the garden. Straining her muscles to lift the heavy potted plants, she looked under each one, then dug through the damp potting soil with her fingers. All she "discovered" were roots.

Next she scooted over to the white wicker seating arrangement at the opposite end of the balcony. Lying on her back, she slipped under the table and chair, checking to see if the elusive necklace had been taped to the underside of the furniture. That also proved fruitless. Elizabeth swiped her hand across her sweaty forehead. *It must be inside the suite,* she thought.

Her twin was groping through crevices between the couch cushions when Elizabeth stepped back into the sitting room. Suddenly Jessica jerked back her hand and twisted her face into a sour expression. "Yuck, how disgusting!"

"What?" Elizabeth asked.

"Old chewing gum!" Jessica answered. "Can you believe it? This couch is probably worth more than our entire house, and it's loaded with chewing gum!"

"I'm surprised the countess hasn't issued a written complaint," Elizabeth said.

Jessica smirked. "It's probably her gum." She stared at Elizabeth narrowly. "What happened to you?" she asked. "Your face is all muddy."

Elizabeth glanced at her dirty hands and realized she must've smeared herself with potting soil. "The necklace isn't buried in the plants," she remarked dryly.

"You'd better wash that off, or you'll leave dirty fingerprints all over the place," Jessica warned.

Elizabeth nodded and followed her twin into the bathroom that was off the sitting room. "This is really nice," Jessica said wistfully as Elizabeth washed her hands. "It's so unfair that they have *three* bathrooms while we have to share one!"

Next they searched through one of the bedrooms, which was obviously Antonia's. "She certainly is a sicko neat freak," Jessica remarked as she pulled open the top dresser drawer. "Worse than you, Liz."

Curious, Elizabeth peered over Jessica's shoulder and chuckled. Antonia's socks and underwear were folded and lined up in neat, color-coordinated rows. "You're right," Elizabeth remarked.

After they'd made a thorough sweep of Antonia's room, they checked out the countess's. Elizabeth searched through the clothes in the free-standing oak wardrobe, slipping her hand into each pocket. All she found was a used handkerchief and a roll of mints.

Elizabeth heard her twin gasp. Jessica was

kneeling on the floor in front of an open metal box. "Look what I found, Liz!"

"A diamond necklace?" Elizabeth asked hopefully, rushing to her side. She saw what was inside the box and slumped disappointedly. It was filled with candy bars, some of them partially eaten.

"I'll bet it's the countess's personal, secret stash," Jessica remarked with a giggle. "She's a closet junk-food addict. Now we can blackmail her."

Elizabeth glared at her twin mildly. "That's a *great* idea, Jessica," she muttered sarcastically.

Suddenly Jessica's face turned pale. "What was that?" she whispered.

Elizabeth perked her ears and heard it too—the sound of footsteps approaching the suite. Then the outer door opened, and someone entered the sitting room. Elizabeth's heart stopped, frozen. The twins exchanged wide-eyed looks of alarm.

Jessica soundlessly eased the metal box shut and slipped it into the bottom dresser drawer. "Let's hide!" she breathed.

Forcing back a feeling of cold panic, Elizabeth flattened herself on the floor and shimmied faceup under the bed with Jessica. An instant later the bedroom door burst open and someone entered. Elizabeth turned her head slightly and saw two feet in white leather pumps standing next to the bed. She recognized those shoes immediately.

Elizabeth's heart stopped. *It's the countess!* she realized. *We're trapped!*

Chapter 9

Elizabeth felt as if her heart were lodged in her throat as she and Jessica lay motionless in their hiding place under the countess's bed. The bed sagged closer to their faces, indicating that the countess had plunked herself down on the mattress. Then Elizabeth heard the phone handset being picked up, followed by the countess's haughty voice.

"Yes, the arrangements have been made for a smooth transaction," she said firmly. "But I suggest we move quickly. There may be complications . . . outside elements. . . ."

Jessica squeezed Elizabeth's hand.

"This has been planned carefully to the very last detail," the countess continued. "I won't tolerate any intervention at this point." With that she hung up and marched out of the suite, slamming the door behind her.

Elizabeth closed her eyes and took a deep breath. "That was way too close," she whispered shakily.

The twins squirmed out from under the bed and brushed themselves off. "What did you think about that phone call?" Jessica said. "I'll bet she was making arrangements to fence the stolen necklace and the heirloom she claims to have lost on the train too. By the way, do you know what the heirloom is? I couldn't understand what everyone was saying on the train."

Elizabeth shook her head. "I don't think anyone on the train mentioned what sort of an object it was." She gazed around the room and frowned. "But let's face it, Jess, the countess hasn't hidden the diamond necklace in this suite. It could be anywhere. We may never find it."

"We'll just have to keep looking," Jessica insisted.

Elizabeth sighed wearily. "This castle is bigger than the Sweet Valley Mall," she pointed out discouragingly. "And that's not including the miles of secret passageways under the château."

Jessica's face lit up. "Of course, the secret passageways! Let's get Jacques to help us. He knows them very well." She grinned mischievously. "That's how he sneaks in to see me."

Elizabeth shook her head. "I've been down there with Laurent," she said. "It's totally dark, and there must be trillions of nooks and crannies where a person could hide a necklace. We'd never be able to search every inch of the passageways even if we spent the entire summer down there."

"We'll just have to stay close to the countess and wait for her to lead us to the treasure," Jessica suggested as they crept out of the suite.

"I'm sure she'll love that," Elizabeth replied sarcastically.

Jessica snickered. "I still think we should ask Jacques to help us," she said. "He's very resourceful."

Elizabeth grimaced inwardly. She didn't care how resourceful Jacques Landeau might be or how much Jessica gushed about him and the bracelet he'd given her. Something about the guy made Elizabeth uneasy.

Jacques uttered a low, sleepy groan as he opened his eyes Friday morning. He found himself twisted uncomfortably in a tight, dark space, and for one frightening moment he couldn't remember how he'd gotten there. When he tried to move, a quick, hot pain shot up and down his left leg, shocking him fully awake. Suddenly it all came back to him.

Le Château d'Amour Inconnu, he realized. He'd fallen asleep in the linen closet near Jessica's room. He had no idea what time it was. There was a shaft of light shining under the closet door, so it was probably well after daybreak. That meant he'd spent the entire night there. *I must be getting soft in the head,* Jacques chided himself.

He flexed his left foot and winced at the sudden burst of pins and needles. He reached down and rubbed it vigorously to get the blood circulating, then stretched his neck from side to side to ease the stiffness.

His father had been pleased when Jacques had presented him with the diamond necklace. "This fine bonus will set us up for the entire winter," Louis had said proudly. Then he had asked for the emerald.

Jacques cringed with remorse as he recalled his father's expression when he'd told him that he didn't have it. It was as if Louis Landeau had aged years in a matter of seconds—his eyes had turned glassy, and the worry lines on his face had deepened. Jacques had promised to bring him the emerald that weekend—without fail.

He had sneaked into the château the previous evening and had been about to enter Jessica's room when a flock of servants had come running up the stairs. That's when Jacques had ducked into the linen closet. By the time the corridor cleared, Jessica had gone to her room. Jacques had decided to wait until she was asleep. He'd peeked out from the linen closet every few minutes to see if she'd turned off her light. But apparently she'd outlasted him, and he'd fallen asleep without getting the emerald.

I won't let it happen again, Jacques resolved firmly. Taking a deep breath, he shifted onto his hands and knees and crawled out of his hiding spot behind a stack of folded sheets. He eased the door open slightly and peered through the crack. Several maids were set up with ladders and buckets at both ends of the corridor, washing the tall windows.

Frustrated, Jacques cursed under his breath as he closed the door. The windows were large, with dozens of wood-framed panes in each, all of which had to be washed individually. The job could take hours.

Jacques grabbed a stack of towels and made himself a cushioned seat on the floor. *I might as well make myself comfortable,* he thought wryly.

"The costumes are supposed to be grouped by size, but things have become disorganized in here," Anna explained as she ushered Jessica, Elizabeth, and the children into the wardrobe room after breakfast.

Jessica looked around, impressed. More than a dozen wardrobes were lined up along the walls. The large bay window at the far end of the room was flanked on either side by makeup tables with lighted mirrors. *I'd like a closet like this someday,* she thought.

"This room, it is used often during the summer," Anna commented. "The princess enjoys hosting lavish costume parties impromptu. On several occasions more than thirty guests are in here at once, scrambling to find the most outlandish outfit of all. Sometimes the parties never leave this room, and we end up serving the buffet on the makeup tables."

"Sounds wild," Jessica muttered.

Anna pointed out the wardrobes where they might find costumes for the children. "The ball gowns are in here," she said, indicating the wardrobe nearest the door. "Help yourself to something nice to wear after the tableau. The dressing rooms are through there." She pointed to a door on the right.

"This is going to be such fun!" Jessica exclaimed.

"I hope so," Anna replied. "Though I'll be glad when it's all over and I can soak for an entire day in a hot bath." Anna turned to the children. "You will behave nicely and do what you're told, yes?"

"Yes!" they shouted enthusiastically.

Elizabeth and Jessica looked at each other and laughed. "Promises, promises," Jessica muttered.

"I want to wear a costume like a tree," Pierre announced. "Or a tiger."

Claudine had already opened one of the wardrobes and was fondling the corner of a green velvet gown. "I want this one," she said. "I want to look like the beautiful girl in the bluebird story."

Manon jumped up and raised her hands in the air. "I want to look like a grand elephant!"

"Let's pick the story theme for our tableau," Elizabeth suggested.

"I want the bluebird story," Claudine announced.

Jessica shrugged. "It's not a very well-known story," she pointed out. "We should probably pick something that would be easier to guess. We do want our team to win, right?"

The children cheered excitedly.

"OK, so what about *Sleeping Beauty* or *Cinderella*?" Elizabeth suggested.

Claudine's eyes widened. "*Cinderella!* I love *Cinderella.*"

"Me too!" Manon said.

Pierre rolled his eyes dramatically. "Girls!" he grumbled.

Jessica and Elizabeth cracked up at his expression. "I think you'd be perfect as the prince's footman," Elizabeth said.

"What's that?" he asked.

"He's the guy who tries the magic slipper on the feet of all the maidens in the kingdom," Elizabeth answered.

Pierre didn't seem too impressed. Jessica ruffled his curly hair. "Come on, it's a fun job, Pierre. You get to shove that glass slipper on all those ugly feet. . . ."

Pierre sighed melodramatically. "All right," he agreed. "Let's do *Cinderella.*"

"Claudine can be Cinderella," Elizabeth said. "Jess, would you rather be the wicked stepmother or the fairy godmother?"

"The fairy godmother, of course," Jessica replied.

"Could I be *l'éléphant?*" Manon pleaded.

"Elephant?" Jessica asked, glancing at her twin for verification.

Elizabeth nodded and squatted down to Manon's eye level. "I'm afraid there aren't any elephants in *Cinderella*. You could be a wicked stepsister," she offered.

Manon tipped her head from side to side, chanting, "Wicked stepsister," over and over.

"I think that's a yes," Jessica said cheerfully. "Now that we've got our theme, let's have some fun!"

They decided to create the scene where Prince Charming's footman was slipping the glass slipper onto Cinderella's foot. For the next hour they flitted around the room excitedly, poking through all the wardrobes and trying on item after item.

After some digging Jessica found a clear plastic sandal in a box of odds and ends. "I found our glass slipper," she announced proudly. "There's only one in here, though, and it's way too big for Claudine, but that shouldn't matter for the tableau."

"It's perfect," Elizabeth agreed. "What do you think of this dress?" She held up a full-length beaded shift in a severe shade of mustard brown. It was chic, elegant, glamorous, and yet matronly drab at the same time.

"It's awesome!" Jessica exclaimed. "*Exactly* what a wicked stepmother would wear."

Jessica tried on several potential outfits that would suit a fairy godmother. She finally spotted a pale green silk gown with silver threads woven through the fabric. "This is the one," she whispered excitedly as she took it off its hanger.

"That's beautiful," Elizabeth said when Jessica walked out of the dressing room wearing the gown.

143

"And I found a lace shawl we can use to make your veil." She sat Jessica down at one of the makeup stools. "Let me try something."

Jessica watched in the mirror as Elizabeth twisted her hair into a topknot. She anchored the veil with some hairpins, draping it across the lower half of her face.

"What do you think?" Elizabeth asked.

Jessica narrowed her eyes and turned from side to side as she studied her reflection. "Needs height," she said.

Elizabeth pursed her lips. "You're right. Hold on, I've got an idea. . . ."

Claudine skipped over to the makeup table, holding up the hem of the long pink dress she was wearing. "You're beautiful, Mademoiselle Jessica," she murmured.

Jessica grinned. "Thanks." She looked over Claudine's outfit and nodded. The dress had lots of lace trim, a high waist, and puffy sleeves. "You look very pretty yourself, kid," she said.

Elizabeth returned a moment later with a roll of toilet paper in her hand. Jessica glared at her. "What are you planning to do with that?"

"Put it on your head," she answered. She stuck her fingers into the hollow center of the roll and rotated it around her opposite hand, wrapping the tissue around her wrist.

Jessica snorted. "I don't know how to break it to you, Liz. But I'm not the sort of person who

144

wears *toilet paper* as a fashion accessory."

"Trust me," Elizabeth insisted. "And sit still." She gathered the entire length of toilet paper around her hand and set it aside. Then she redid Jessica's hair, using the empty cardboard roll as a frame. Then she arranged the lace veil over her creation, and the effect was totally stunning.

Jessica smiled broadly. "Liz, you're a genius!" The delicate veil seemed to float down the sides of her face like a pale green cloud. Jessica knew she looked lovely, but not quite as glamorous as she'd hoped. She frowned. *It needs . . . something,* she decided.

"What's wrong?" Elizabeth asked.

"I don't know." Jessica shrugged. "It seems rather . . . *plain.*" Suddenly a brilliant idea popped into her head. "I have the perfect solution!" she cried, bolting from the chair.

"Where are you going?" Elizabeth asked.

"I have to get something from my room," she replied over her shoulder. "I'll be right back."

Finally! Jacques mumbled to himself as he slipped out of the linen closet into the deserted hallway. He'd feared that those maids would never leave. At one point he'd overheard them complaining that all the servants' rooms were going to be searched by the police later that day.

Thank goodness the emerald will be long gone from the château before that *happens,* he thought. Otherwise Jessica would be blamed for its theft.

Jacques crept into her room and made his way over to her bed, stepping over the junk strewn across her floor. A gentle smile tugged at the corners of his lips. She was even messier than he was!

Jacques tried not to think about Jessica . . . but her face floated into his mind's eye. She would hate him forever when she discovered the emerald missing. *If only* . . . Jacques shook his head to clear it. Their love had been doomed from the moment he'd stepped off the train. Wishing that they might have a future would only cause him more pain. His father needed him, and Jacques would never let him down . . . even if it meant giving up the most wonderful girl in the entire world.

Jacques raised a corner of her pillow and grabbed the red velvet case underneath it. His hands trembled as he raised the lid. The emerald pendant was inside, glimmering in the bright sunlight that filtered into the room. Sighing with relief, Jacques snapped the lid shut and slipped it into the pocket of his jeans.

Suddenly the door opened. He jerked his head around and gasped, his heart stuck in his throat. "Jessica!" he uttered breathlessly.

Chapter 10

"Jacques!" Jessica gasped in pleased surprise. She quickly shut her bedroom door, then whirled around to face him. He was wearing a black shirt that accentuated his dark eyes and broad shoulders—and he looked absolutely gorgeous. Jessica's heart skipped a beat, and her mouth went dry.

Jacques appeared equally shaken at the sight of her, his brown eyes wide and luminous. His face was flushed, and his hands were trembling.

"You're here!" Jessica exclaimed breathlessly as she rushed to him.

But Jacques kept her at arm's distance with his hands on her shoulders. He stared at her in awe, his gaze moving slowly from her head down to her feet, then up to her eyes. "You appear like *un ange!*"

"This is my costume for the tableau," Jessica replied with a giggle. "I almost forgot I was wearing it."

"It is very beautiful," he whispered reverently. "*You're* beautiful."

Beaming proudly, Jessica turned from side to side. "I'm supposed to be the fairy godmother in *Cinderella.*"

He reached for her hand and brought it to his lips. "I love you, Jessica."

Jessica gave him a tender smile. "I love you too, Jacques."

Jacques kissed the back of her hand, then clasped it between both of his. A sad, wistful look came into his eyes. "Please, in the future days . . . ," he began, "know that it is forever I love you."

Jessica's heart instantly melted. Tears spilled down her cheeks. "Me too," she replied. "*Forever.*" She leaned toward him and slipped her arms around his waist. Jacques hugged her tightly, whispering French words into her ear.

Suddenly, behind his back, Jessica felt a box-shaped object sticking out of his pocket. An alarm went off in her head. She wondered if Jacques had made another attempt to take back the emerald pendant. *No, he wouldn't do that,* she thought. *Would he?* She had to know for sure.

If this is my jewelry case, Jacques is dead! she fumed as she yanked the suspicious rectangle out of his pocket.

In the span of a heartbeat Jessica jumped away from Jacques and glanced at what she'd taken. As she'd feared, it was her red jewelry case. She raised the lid and saw that the pendant was inside.

Jessica snapped the case shut. Anger and confusion coursed through her as she faced Jacques. "Why don't you want me to have this?" she asked him.

Jacques lowered his eyes, his expression heavy with guilt. "You deserve only the real gems, not an inexpensive fake like that one."

Jessica gritted her teeth. "How many times do I have to tell you that I don't care about that? Fake or not, I love this pendant because it was a gift from you."

Jacques faced her squarely. "I'm ashamed to have given you such a cheap gift."

"Get over it!" she spat.

Jacques sighed wearily and lowered himself to the edge of the bed. "I don't understand how could a sophisticated, elegant girl as you become so attached to such a garish piece of junk."

Jessica opened the case and gazed at the pendant. "I think it's lovely," she argued.

Jacques uttered a derisive sound. "It is worthless."

Jessica shut the jewelry case and glared at him. "I think it's precious."

Jacques shook his head. "You are wrong!" he cried vehemently. "That is a thing for the garbage."

Jessica squared her shoulders and raised her chin. "Well, I feel differently," she said. "And if you can't respect my feelings, then there's nothing more for us to say to each other."

Jacques moved toward her, his arms open and

his eyes pleading. "Jessica, *mon ange* . . . it is only because you are ignorant that you treasure this meaningless scrap."

Jessica's temper exploded like an angry volcano. "*Ignorant?* How *dare* you!" she raged at him. "I never want to see you again."

Not bothering to wait for Jacques's reaction, she rushed out of her room, tears streaming down her face.

"Maybe you should tell the de Sainte-Maries about Jacques's visits," Elizabeth advised Jessica as they headed toward their rooms that evening. "With everything that's going on, it might be best if they knew."

Jessica sniffed. "I couldn't," she replied glumly. "As mad as I am at him, I still don't want to cause a major problem for his family."

Elizabeth glanced at her twin, noting the dark red circles around her eyes. Jessica had hardly stopped crying for more than five minutes since her blowup with Jacques.

I'd love to wring his neck! Elizabeth thought fiercely, clenching her fists at her side. She'd known all along that he would eventually hurt Jessica.

"I'm not going to let him ruin the weekend for me," Jessica declared. "Our tableau is going to be fantastic. And who knows . . . maybe I'll snag a handsome prince at the ball."

Elizabeth smiled. "You're something else, Jess," she teased gently.

Jessica looped her arm around Elizabeth's neck. "If my own sister is dating a prince, why should I settle for a duke?"

Elizabeth rolled her eyes, amazed at her twin's bizarre logic. "Things aren't exactly settled between Laurent and me," she pointed out cautiously. "I haven't even seen him since Wednesday."

"I have," Jessica replied.

Elizabeth raised her eyebrows at that. "When?"

"Yesterday," Jessica answered breezily. "He came to the château for the family photograph. I only caught a glimpse of him. He was wearing a fancy dark blue uniform with all sorts of medals on the jacket." She shot Elizabeth a sly grin and added, "He looked totally *hot!*"

Elizabeth felt a warm rush of emotion. "I wish I'd seen him," she murmured.

"You will at the ball," Jessica pointed out excitedly. "And I expect you to make him introduce me to all his royal buddies . . . the good-looking ones anyway."

Elizabeth laughed. "I'll see what I can do." But her smile instantly faded as they entered the servants' wing.

Maids were scurrying through the first-floor corridor, obviously upset, slamming doors, uttering protests about the way they were being treated. Some were even threatening to quit their jobs.

Elizabeth felt a sinking sensation in her gut. "I wonder what's going on now."

Jessica snorted. "Whatever it is, I'll bet the countess had something to do with it."

Elizabeth caught sight of Brigitte, the maid who worked in the kitchen. "What's wrong?" she asked.

Brigitte threw up her hands and shrieked, *"Une disgrâce!"*

Elizabeth frowned. "What's a disgrace?"

"They search our rooms!" Brigitte replied in English. "The police!"

"That's outrageous!" Elizabeth said. She and Jessica ran upstairs to check their own rooms.

Elizabeth opened her door and her heart plummeted. All her drawers were open, her clothes in disarray. Her blanket and sheets had been pushed to the foot of the bed. The pillow was on the floor. The contents of her canvas bag had been dumped out and strewn across the dresser top. "I can't believe this!" Elizabeth fumed. The very idea of strangers going through her personal belongings made her sick.

She went across the hall and knocked on her twin's door. Jessica opened it and waved her in. "I'm so mad I could scream," Elizabeth muttered through clenched teeth.

Then she looked around and uttered a horrified gasp. "Oh, Jessica . . . how terrible!" she cried. "They really tore up your room!"

Jessica shrugged. "Actually I'm not even sure if

anyone's been in here. No, wait . . ." She walked over to the dresser and picked up a bottle of nail polish. "They were here, all right. I haven't seen Malibu Mauve since the bottle fell behind the dresser three days ago."

Elizabeth sat down on the corner of Jessica's bed and folded her arms tightly. "I agree that this is probably all the countess's doing. I just wish the de Sainte-Maries would send her and her nasty daughter packing!"

"Don't worry," Jessica replied. "When we find the di Riminis' missing jewels and bust that witch for insurance fraud . . . we'll have our sweet revenge!"

The following morning Jessica sensed a strange atmosphere brewing in the château as she and Elizabeth supervised the children's breakfast in the kitchen. Although the entire staff was busy working on the final preparations for the evening's festivities, the household seemed unnaturally calm. It was as if a temporary cease-fire had been declared in honor of the royal ball.

After breakfast the twins brought the children back to the wardrobe room for a dress rehearsal of their tableau. "Manon, sit still," Jessica ordered as she drew a big, ugly mole on the little girl's chin.

"But it tickles," Manon complained.

Jessica stepped back and admired her work. With bright red lipstick and her eyes circled in heavy brown eye shadow, Manon looked almost

153

frightening. "You're a perfect wicked stepsister," she pronounced, turning the chair so that Manon could see herself in the mirror.

Manon's jaw dropped. Then she raised her hands, her fingers curled like claws, and growled at her reflection. "I'm like a monster!"

Jessica laughed. "Only when you miss your afternoon nap," she replied jokingly. She uncapped the eyebrow pencil again. "I think you need one more black mole, right on your nose. . . ."

Claudine came barreling out of the dressing room with Pierre right behind her, both of them in full costume. "Give it back!" he was hollering.

Jessica's hand slipped. Instead of a mole Manon now had a jagged black line on her nose. "What's going on!" Jessica demanded.

"Claudine took the glass slipper," Pierre cried. "But *I* am the foot guy."

"We don't have time to fool around, guys," she warned. "Claudine, give him back the shoe, and why isn't your hair done yet?"

Jessica glanced over at her twin. Elizabeth was sitting at the makeup table, staring absently at nothing.

Jessica exhaled an exasperated sigh. "Earth to Liz!" she called tauntingly. "We have a tableau to win—*remember?*"

Elizabeth blinked. "Oh, right," she mumbled. "Come here, Claudine." Reaching for a comb, she knocked over an open jar of hairpins, scattering them across the table.

Jessica rolled her eyes. She knew exactly why her sister had suddenly turned into a scatter-brained ditz. Falling in love with Laurent had shaken Elizabeth's neat, orderly, *dull* world. *Thank goodness I talked her into coming to Château d'Amour Inconnu,* Jessica thought. *If it weren't for me, Liz would probably live her entire life in a permanent rut!*

When the children were finally ready, the twins slipped into their costumes. Jessica stood before a three-sided full-length mirror, admiring herself from different angles. The emerald pendant was the crowning touch—literally. She'd looped the chain around the tall chignon on top of her head, with the shimmering green stone adorning her forehead. *I look absolutely amazing,* she decided. She felt a sudden, sad twinge as she remembered how awed Jacques had been at seeing her in costume—just before she'd discovered her jewelry case in his pocket.

Jessica clenched her jaw as a wave of fresh pain crashed over her. *I'm sure he'll be back,* she thought. *And maybe he'll have finally learned that he can't dictate my feelings and opinions!*

"Let's get in position," Elizabeth called for attention.

They practiced holding the scene over and over, gradually working up to the five minutes that would be required during the actual game. Jessica was amazed by the children's serious attitude and excellent behavior.

After the rehearsal the twins turned their attention to what everyone would wear to the ball. They decided Pierre and Claudine could wear their costumes to the ball, but Manon's drab gray shift wouldn't do at all. Jessica found her a pink party dress, with flounces and satin bows along the hem. Manon was thrilled.

For herself Jessica selected a sleeveless lavender gown with delicate lace trim on the shoulder straps. Standing in front of the mirror in the dressing room, Jessica held the emerald pendant up to her neck to study the effect.

Jacques had called his gift "cheap" and "garish." *Will everyone at the ball think I'm cheap and garish if I wear this?* Jessica worried.

Just then she heard the sound of fluttering fabric coming from one of the dressing stalls, followed by her twin's muffled curse. Jessica frowned. *What is Elizabeth doing in there?* she wondered as she went to investigate.

She found Elizabeth struggling with a monstrous red velvet gown heavily trimmed with gold piping. Her hair was in wild disarray, and beads of perspiration dripped down the sides of her face. "Who's winning?" Jessica asked dryly. "My bet's on the dress."

Elizabeth shot her a withering glare. "Very funny!"

Jessica turned her sister around and saw a hidden row of buttons at the waist. "No wonder," she said as she began unfastening them. "Elizabeth, you're going to have to get ahold of yourself. You're acting like a total airhead, and it's driving me crazy."

"I know," Elizabeth breathed. "But I'm so nervous about everything . . . the ball tonight . . . Laurent. . . . Everything is so complicated all of a sudden. Plus I keeping thinking back to what happened between Todd and me. . . ."

How can she even remember boring-as-cold-toast Todd Wilkins when she has Laurent? Jessica wondered incredulously. She finished unbuttoning the gown, turned her sister around, and looked her in the eye. "Liz, you love Laurent, and he loves you, right? That doesn't sound too complicated to me at all."

Elizabeth chewed her bottom lip. "Maybe it would help if I could talk things over with him before the ball."

"That's a great idea!" Jessica replied enthusiastically.

Elizabeth glanced at her watch. "Laurent is probably at the cottage right now."

"Go see him," Jessica insisted. "We're pretty much finished here, and the kids will be taking a nap soon."

"You sure you don't mind?" Elizabeth asked.

Jessica rolled her eyes. "What I *mind* is having an air-brain twin who can't concentrate on anything for more than two seconds! And if you don't do something to put your mind at rest, I'm going to strangle you before the day is over."

Elizabeth smiled tremulously. "When you put it

that way, I don't seem to have much choice."

Jessica grinned. "None at all," she replied. "Now let's get you out of that ridiculous gown. It makes you look like a couch!"

Laurent cringed at the sound of Antonia's horsey giggle as they sat side by side in the garden behind his cottage. *Is that what I have to put up with for the rest of my life?* he wondered. Sitting directly across from him in a patio chair, the countess di Rimini shot daggers at him with her burning green eyes, as if she'd read his mind.

"You're not offended that I chose Giaccomo Monattini to design the bridal gowns, are you, Laurent?" Antonia was asking. She spoke French, overpronouncing each word as if she were onstage.

Laurent blinked, nonplussed. He didn't have a clue as to what she was saying. Last he knew, she'd been describing the quirky habits of her grandmother . . . or cousin. Apparently he'd lost track of the conversation.

Antonia whinnied again, setting his teeth on edge. "You are offended, aren't you!" she said teasingly. "Just because he's not French. Aren't you the stubborn one!" Her clammy fingers gripped his palm. "The honeymoon will be in France, of course. I flatly turned down the invitation to Laestra, not that I wouldn't have loved to go. It's so beautiful this time of year. But I absolutely loathe Princess Charlotte. . . ."

Laurent's eyes narrowed at the mention of his childhood friend. Princess Charlotte of Laestra was one of the nicest, kindest, and most intelligent people he knew. In many ways she reminded him of Elizabeth.

". . . And furthermore, she is one girl who should never wear red. She looked absolutely hideous. I told her that, but of course she wouldn't listen." Antonia grinned nastily. "I'm not one to listen to gossip, but I heard Princess Charlotte was recently seen in a Paris nightclub with a gang of American college students!"

The countess shuddered dramatically. "Americans are notorious for trying to wedge their way into noble society."

"Apparently Princess Charlotte met those lowlifes during her recent visit to New York City." Antonia sniffed loudly. "And she had the nerve to snub *me* in Monte Carlo last month! I wish we didn't have to invite her to the wedding, Mummy," she pouted.

"King Josef of Laestra is a dear friend of your father's," the countess said.

Laurent caught himself staring at a white dove that had touched down on the rose arbor. It brought to his mind the legend of the Château d'Amour Inconnu and the brokenhearted lovers who'd lost each other forever. For as long as he could remember, the story had symbolized for him the aura of mystery and romance surrounding the château.

But now the legend filled him with resentment. It had come to represent the traditions and heritage Laurent had been born into, which now demanded that he follow in the footsteps of Prince Frédéric the Third and give up his true love for the sake of duty and honor. *I'm doomed to live the legend—no, the* curse—*of the Château d'Amour Inconnu,* Laurent thought, his heart sinking with despair.

Antonia elbowed him in the side, startling him. Laurent stared at her blankly.

"I said a ski honeymoon will be such fun, don't you agree?" Antonia asked. "My uncle's chalet in Chamonix will be ours for as long as we care to stay. I just love skiing in the Alps. . . ."

Laurent's mind wandered off again. *I wonder if Elizabeth likes to ski. . . .*

A firm tap on his shoulder jolted him back to the present. He realized the countess had smacked him with her fan.

"You look tired, dear," she said to him. "Shall I go inside and fix some tea?"

"No!" Laurent blurted. He exhaled deeply and pushed his fingers through his hair. "What I mean is . . . it's very kind of you to offer, but no, thank you."

"It would help you stay awake," the countess persisted.

Laurent cringed at the thought of that woman in his cottage, rummaging around in his kitchen . . . where Elizabeth had prepared coffee for him only a few days earlier. . . .

A dull ache squeezed his heart. *There's no way I'll let them inside!* he vowed silently. He knew it was ridiculous, but he felt that if he opened up his cottage to the countess and Antonia, it would somehow diminish the memories he cherished of Elizabeth's visits.

"Don't worry, I'll stay awake," Laurent assured them, silently adding, *no matter what.*

Elizabeth hurried through the topiary maze toward Laurent's cottage. Created during the twelfth century, the huge labyrinth was one of the largest in Europe. Elizabeth had gotten lost in it on previous occasions—and had ended up at Laurent's cottage each time.

Maybe he really is my destiny, Elizabeth thought. *But am I ready for a relationship that will change my entire life?* She thought back to the conversation she'd overheard between Henri and the maids on Wednesday night. They'd said Laurent's engagement would be announced at the ball.

Elizabeth shook her head. *I must have misunderstood,* she decided. *Laurent wouldn't ask me to marry him in front of hundreds of strangers. He's much too considerate to turn such a private moment into a public spectacle.* But she knew she wouldn't have a moment of peace until she talked everything over with him.

Elizabeth was surprised—and disappointed—to hear voices as she drew nearer to the cottage. She had counted on Laurent's being alone. For a moment she considered turning around. *Oh, well, I've come this far,* she thought, pushing herself forward.

Elizabeth stepped out of the maze . . . and her heart plummeted.

Laurent was sitting in the garden, holding Antonia's hand.

Chapter 11

Elizabeth's jaw dropped. Time seemed to stand still, freezing the scene in the cottage garden into a horrible tableau. In the span of a heartbeat a myriad of impressions flooded her brain.

Laurent and Antonia were seated side by side under the rose arbor, holding hands. He had on a dark pin-striped suit, with a pale blue shirt and gray tie.

Antonia was wearing a blue dress, pearl necklace, and black pumps. Her red hair had been arranged in a tight French braid. A few rose petals and dry leaves were scattered on the ground by their feet. The countess was there too, watching the couple with a smug, calculating look on her face. Her hands were clasped on her lap, the deep ruffles of her pink blouse falling across her knuckles.

Elizabeth shook her head, trying to understand what her eyes were seeing. *Laurent loves* me . . . *but he's holding* Antonia's *hand.* . . .

Suddenly the truth hit Elizabeth like a splash of ice water in her face. *Antonia is his fiancée,* she realized. It was *their* engagement that would be announced at the ball that evening.

What a fool I was to think he was going to propose to me! she thought, giving herself a firm mental kick. Her gaze zeroed in on Laurent's and Antonia's clasped hands resting on the bench between them.

A sharp pain stabbed Elizabeth's heart. She couldn't believe Laurent had deceived her so cruelly. *And with Antonia of all people!* she fumed as she yanked a green bud off the hedges and threw it on the ground. *Was I nothing more than a fun pastime for him while he waited for his engagement to be announced?*

Her anger at its boiling point, Elizabeth strode forward with her hands clenched at her sides. "Did it occur to you even *once* that maybe you should let me *know* you're engaged?" she raged at Laurent.

Everyone turned to her with startled looks on their faces. Laurent immediately dropped Antonia's hand and jumped to his feet. "Elizabeth."

The countess glared at him. "Obviously your family's little au pair girl has taken your attentions toward her too seriously, Your Highness," she said in French. Elizabeth understood every word.

Antonia moved to stand beside Laurent. Looping her arm through his, she gave Elizabeth an insulting up-and-down stare, then turned to her mother. *"Americans,"* she remarked, rolling her eyes.

"I'm proud of what I am," Elizabeth shot back.

The countess laughed coldly and addressed her in English. "Pride won't change your place in society. Only an American could fail to notice the difference between royalty and commoners," she said. "Imagine a prince, a man of worth, taking someone like you seriously."

Elizabeth's temper flashed dangerously. Spots of red seemed to glitter before her eyes, and her nerves were pumped for battle. "How dare you!" she spat furiously.

She glanced at Laurent and realized he wasn't going to say a single word in her defense. He wouldn't even look at her. *Isn't what we shared worth fighting for?* she silently fumed.

Her heart pounded as she waited for him to say or do something to let the di Rimini hags know that he wasn't one of them . . . that he loved and respected Elizabeth even though she wasn't of noble birth.

The seconds ticked by, and still Laurent hadn't made a move. Elizabeth crumpled inwardly as all the fight seeped out of her. She felt abandoned and defeated. *Laurent isn't on my side,* she thought, her heart shattering to pieces. Choking back a sob, she turned and ran out of the garden.

Laurent stared after Elizabeth, panic mounting

inside him. *Don't let her go!* his mind screamed.

Unable to stop himself, he freed his arm from Antonia's tight grip and took off running. "Elizabeth, wait!" he called urgently.

He caught up to her just before she reached the maze. "I love you, Elizabeth," he swore as he swept her up in his arms. "You have to believe me."

"Why, Laurent?" she sobbed. "Why should I believe anything you say?"

Laurent wove his fingers through her silky blond hair and gently tilted her head back so that they were gazing at each other directly. "Because it's the truth," he declared simply.

"Laurent—" Elizabeth pressed a corner of her bottom lip between her teeth. "At the Château d'Amour Inconnu, I'm considered an inferior being, along with my sister and the rest of the servants. *That's* the truth. And it'll never change."

"Neither will the way I feel about you." He pressed his lips against hers and put his whole heart into a deep, searing kiss.

Laurent heard the countess's shrill voice calling him. *My duty,* he groaned to himself. He remembered how much was at stake—the honor of his family and his future as a leader. But giving up his own happiness seemed too high a price.

Elizabeth abruptly ended the kiss. As if she sensed the conflict inside him, she gazed up at him with a question in her eyes.

Laurent felt as though a jagged blade were

bisecting his heart. He longed to put Elizabeth's mind to rest and reassure her that they could have a future together. But that would mean turning his back on his father—which Laurent wasn't willing to do. Elizabeth exhaled shakily. Tears filled her eyes, spilling in streams down her face. She jerked away from him and turned to go.

Laurent watched her disappear into the maze. A cold, empty sensation enveloped him. *I've just lost the only girl I've ever loved,* he realized sadly.

"Laurent!" the countess bellowed impatiently.

Laurent closed his eyes and clenched his jaw. "Duty and honor," he reminded himself under his breath as he headed back to the garden. *No matter how painful,* he added silently.

I never meant for this to happen, Jessica thought as her twin sobbed in her arms that evening. They were sitting on the couch in the nursery, away from the guests and servants buzzing around in the main areas of the château. Jessica had brought up the costumes from the wardrobe room and had laid out everything they would need for the tableau. They had less than an hour to get ready, but Elizabeth's tears showed no sign of easing up anytime soon.

Jessica swallowed against the thickening lump in her throat. She felt as if she were being choked by her own guilt and remorse. If she had told Elizabeth about Antonia and Laurent's engagement from the very start, her twin wouldn't be suffering a broken heart. *But Elizabeth and Laurent were supposed to get together and live happily ever after,* Jessica argued silently in her own defense.

Claudine came over to the couch, waving her pink sash like a banner. "I can't tie this to me," she said.

"I'll help you in minute," Jessica whispered. She glanced over at the other two children. Manon huddled in a corner, sucking her thumb, with a sad look on her face. Pierre was sitting at the table, playing with his plastic miniature soldiers. Jessica had managed to get the children changed into their costumes, but they still had to have their makeup and hair done. They would need to hurry to be ready on time.

"Elizabeth, listen to me," Jessica began in a gentle but firm tone. "The tableau starts in less than an hour." She leaned back and looked her twin in the eye. "Are we going to drop out of the game?" Jessica asked.

Elizabeth's eyes were puffy and red from crying. She drew in a shuddering breath, her chin quivering. "I can't believe what a fool I was," she sobbed.

Jessica gave her shoulders a brief shake. "Don't think about that right now. We have to get ready for the tableau."

"They were holding hands!" Elizabeth wailed. Fresh tears cascaded down her cheeks. "Why wasn't he honest with me from the beginning?"

Jessica flinched. *Why wasn't I honest with her from the beginning?*

Elizabeth hiccuped sharply. "I just want to go back to Sweet Valley."

"No, you don't," Jessica countered gently.

"I do," Elizabeth said with a shuddering gasp.

Jessica shook her head. "Elizabeth, if we win the tableau, we'll be beating all those royals and nobles at their own game."

Elizabeth sniffed loudly and reached for the tissue box on the side table. "I just can't do it, Jess. I can't face all those people . . . like this."

"Sure, you can," Jessica replied encouragingly.

Elizabeth shook her head and blew her nose. "I just want to stay in my room."

Jessica pressed her bottom lip between her teeth and let out a sharp breath. *I could just punch those di Rimini hags for doing this to Elizabeth,* she thought angrily. *Laurent too, that spineless prince!*

Elizabeth exhaled a shaky breath. "I feel absolutely miserable."

"Think how miserable you'll feel if you let those hags win the tableau," Jessica suggested.

Elizabeth pulled out another tissue and wiped her eyes. "I don't know, Jess. . . ."

Jessica gulped. She hated the idea of forfeiting their chance to win the tableau. But it didn't seem as if she was getting very far with Elizabeth. Jessica decided to appeal to her twin's higher instincts.

"Think of the kids," Jessica said. "They worked

so hard during the rehearsal, and they're so excited. Imagine how crushed they would be if we dropped out."

Elizabeth lowered her eyes and began fiddling with a loose string in her jeans. "I didn't believe they could keep still for minutes at a time."

Jessica felt a small flutter of hope. It was the first nonmiserable thing her twin had said since she'd returned from Laurent's cottage. Maybe her pep talk was working its way through Elizabeth's muddled brain.

"We need you," Jessica pleaded. "You're the only one who knows how to turn a toilet paper roll into an elegant hairstyle," she added jokingly.

The corners of Elizabeth's mouth twitched, as if she were trying to smile.

At that instant Pierre yelled, "Stop!"

Jessica looked over and saw that Claudine had crept under the table and secretly tied his feet together with her pink sash. "Come on, you guys," Jessica pleaded.

Claudine was kneeling next to Pierre's chair, fumbling with the sash. "I can't untie it now," she yelled.

Jessica rolled her eyes and started to get up, but her twin stopped her.

"I'll handle it," Elizabeth offered, her voice suddenly firm and steady as she walked over to the table. "Claudine, you go sit next to Jessica. After I untie your brother, I'm going to do your hair."

"Go, Liz!" Jessica cheered, incredibly relieved.

Elizabeth gave a smile over her shoulder. Her eyes were still red but no longer brimming with hopelessness. "We don't have all day, Jess. Don't you think it's time you got into your fairy god-mother costume?"

Jessica giggled. "She's back, and she's as bossy as ever!" she declared happily.

Kneeling at Pierre's feet, Elizabeth pulled apart the tight knot his sister had tied in the sash. "OK, Miss Cinderella, come here and let me put this around your waist where it belongs," she ordered.

Claudine came bounding over to her. "Is your stomachache all better now?" she asked.

Elizabeth smiled. Jessica's words had stirred her fighting spirit back to life. "My stomach feels fine," she answered. She threaded the sash through the loops around Claudine's dress and tied the ends in a pretty bow. "You're a beautiful Cinderella," she said. "And Pierre is a handsome footman. I'm sure we're going to win the tableau contest."

Claudine and Pierre cheered.

Elizabeth settled them on opposite ends of the couch with a pile of picture books between them and a stern warning to be still.

"Now it's your turn," she said, scooping Manon into her arms. The little girl giggled and hugged Elizabeth's neck.

She dressed Manon in the long gray shift they'd chosen for a stepsister costume, then sat her down at their makeup table. "Mademoiselle Jessica put spots on my nose and made me into a monster," Manon boasted.

"I remember," Elizabeth said as she uncapped a black eyebrow pencil. "And after I put them back on your nose, I'm going to put some on mine."

Elizabeth was brushing dark shadows under Manon's eyes when Jessica returned. "It's my fairy godmother!" Claudine exclaimed.

Jessica executed a graceful pirouette, ending with a deep curtsy.

"You look absolutely beautiful," Elizabeth said.

Jessica took another spin in front of the mirror and smiled at her reflection. "I do, don't I?"

Elizabeth chuckled. "And you're so humble," she teased. She picked up the empty toilet paper roll that was on the table and waved it at Jessica. "Time for your hair appointment, fairy!"

Elizabeth wound her twin's hair around the cardboard cylinder, building it into a sleek, elegant tower. Then, using thick globs of setting gel, she twisted strands of hair around her finger and let them drop along the sides of Jessica's face in delicate, wispy curls.

"That's nice," Elizabeth remarked, stepping back to admire her work. Next she took out Jessica's emerald pendant and secured the chain around the tall chignon with hairpins. Elizabeth carefully arranged the pendant so that the stone draped at the center of Jessica's forehead. "It looks exotic," Elizabeth said.

Jessica looked at the effect in the mirror. "Fairy godmothers tend to be very exotic." She jumped to her feet and waved Elizabeth into the chair. "It's your turn now, wicked stepmother," she announced with a mischievous grin.

"I was just getting to that," Elizabeth murmured. The truth was, she hated the idea of appearing before the de Sainte-Maries and all their guests dressed as the wicked stepmother in an ugly mustard-colored dress and with hideous makeup on her face.

Jessica uncapped a green makeup pencil and began outlining Elizabeth's lips. "You're going to be the ugliest-looking woman to have ever set foot in this château," Jessica promised, then added with a giggle, "well, the third ugliest anyway. I don't think you can ever outdo the countess and Antonia, even with your lips painted green."

Elizabeth chuckled weakly. *I wonder what Laurent will think of me when he sees me in the tableau,* she thought. Her heart ached at the memory of his last kiss, but she refused to let herself fall apart again.

Finally they were all ready. The twins rounded up the children. "Remember, when it's our turn, we have to be perfectly still—just like statues," Elizabeth instructed.

"And Pierre, if you tickle Claudine's foot, I'm going to strangle you," Jessica warned. Elizabeth noticed that her pendant had slipped to the side.

"Just a minute, Jess." Elizabeth grabbed a few more hairpins and, pushing back Jessica's lace veil, anchored the chain around her twin's forehead more securely. "There," she said, adjusting the veil around her sister's face. "I think we're finally ready!"

Chapter 12

Laurent followed Prince Nicolas and Princess Catherine into the makeshift theater in the west wing of the château. All the guests stood up and applauded the royal family.

The convertible walls that normally separated the parlor, the music room, and the library had been rolled back to create a single large space. A platform stage with a red velvet curtain had been set up at one end. There was a door behind it that would allow the presenters to get onstage without being seen by the audience. Strains of music resonated from the end of the room, where the world-famous pianist Lirlyna Kyung was performing on Princess Catherine's Steinway grand piano.

Laurent slouched in his front-row seat, a heavy, dull ache in his gut. He kept replaying that morning's horrible scene in the garden in vivid detail . . .

the tears shimmering in Elizabeth's eyes, the sadness in their blue-green depths . . . the trembling of her soft lips. . . . Laurent hated himself for hurting her. He knew it was wrong not to have been honest with her from the start.

Elizabeth had accused Laurent of deceiving her in order to play a cruel joke on her. But it was himself he'd tried to deceive . . . and if there had been a cruel joke played out, it had been on him.

The professional master of ceremonies hired for the occasion stepped up to the front of the room. After he welcomed everyone on behalf of the de Sainte-Marie family, he officially called for the game to begin. Laurent realized he would see Elizabeth soon, and a burst of excited anticipation shot through him. He would have the luxury of being able to gaze at her for the five-minute span of the tableau.

The lights dimmed, leaving only the spotlights that shone on the stage. Then the red velvet curtain parted to reveal the first tableau, which was presented by Antonia and the countess di Rimini.

Standing on wooden boxes, the two of them were dressed in matching silver evening gowns, with diamond tiaras on their heads and more diamonds around their necks, arms, and ankles. The countess was holding up what looked like a gold baton.

"Dazzling," Laurent heard someone remark. *They certainly are* that, he agreed dryly.

The room buzzed with conversation as the

audience tried to guess the tableau. "The Gemini twins," a man called out.

A woman in the back of the room shouted, "The morning star and the evening star."

"Miss Universe and the first-runner-up," someone else tried. Laurent noticed the countess's expression harden slightly at that guess.

More guesses followed, all of them wrong. When the buzzer finally sounded that the tableau's time was up, there was a collective sigh of relief in the room. The master of ceremonies helped the women step down from the boxes. Laurent could see the fury in the countess's eyes.

"A hint, please?" someone in the audience called out.

The countess raised the baton over her head. "This is my thunderbolt," she said crisply.

"Yes, but who are you?" another person blurted. Several people laughed. Antonia pursed her lips in a sullen pout.

"Please put us out of our mystery, dear ladies, and tell what your tableau depicted," the master of ceremonies said with a bow.

"I am Zeus, and my daughter is Hera," the countess said.

The master of ceremonies nodded blankly. "Please continue your explanation," he said.

The countess glared at him with a haughty look. "From the Greek myth," she replied. "Zeus, the god of the sky, and his wife, Hera."

The audience responded with a few drawn-out "Oh's" and a smattering of applause. "That was going to be my very next guess," a man blurted from the back of the room as the curtain closed.

Laurent knew that Elizabeth's tableau was next. His heart pounded against his chest like a drum. *When the curtain opens again, she will be onstage.*

The next few minutes passed torturously slowly. Laurent nervously drummed his fingers on the arms of his chair, then absently traced one of the swirls in the intricately carved design. Finally the second tableau was announced.

The curtain opened, and there she was. "Elizabeth," Laurent breathed. Focusing only on her, he soaked in every detail—the hideous yellow-brown dress she wore . . . her ramrod posture . . . the matronly hat on her head . . . the laced, pointy-toed boots on her feet. . . . Two dark blemishes had been painted on the side of her nose. Dark smudges circled her eyes. Her lips were colored a ghastly shade of reddish green.

She's absolutely fabulous! Laurent thought. The rest of the audience seemed to agree as they responded enthusiastically to the tableau with praising comments and warm laughter.

Does Elizabeth even know how utterly enchanting she looks on the stage? Laurent wondered. But looking deep into her eyes, he could see how miserable she was. She was obviously struggling valiantly to remain in character.

Laurent swallowed against the thickening in his throat. He was incredibly proud of her . . . and so much in love with her that his heart felt as if it might explode any second.

Elizabeth's hand rested on Manon's shoulder. Both of them were snarling across the stage at Claudine, who, as Cinderella, sat primly on a stool with her legs sticking out. Pierre was kneeling in front of her, holding the glass slipper up to her bare foot.

Laurent chuckled, wondering what threats they'd used to keep Pierre from tickling Claudine's foot.

Jessica, the fairy godmother, was standing behind the stool in a light green gown that shimmered under the lights. Her head was covered with a lace veil, and a large green stone pendant adorned her forehead.

Both sisters were beautiful. But Elizabeth's sweetness and generosity made her irresistibly attractive, even in the role of the wicked stepmother.

Laurent felt a sudden tap on his shoulder. He turned and saw that the countess di Rimini had taken the seat right behind his. "Antonia will be out in a minute," she told him pointedly.

Laurent responded with a slight nod and faced forward, his heart sinking. He was bound by duty and honor to follow the plans that had been carefully arranged for him. His feelings for Elizabeth didn't change a thing. *She's not mine . . . and she never will be,* he reminded himself.

The countess tapped his shoulder again and leaned toward him, stirring up a draft of cloying perfume. "How simpleminded and unsophisticated!" she complained in a raspy whisper. "Leave it to the Americans to present a scene from such a common children's story."

Laurent bristled. "I think they're charming," he retorted.

The countess gripped the back of his chair. "Your young siblings are adorable, of course," she amended. "But those au pair girls . . ." She exhaled a sharp sigh of indignation, fanning Laurent's ear with her stale, hot breath.

Laurent clenched his fists and pressed them into the sides of his chair. "I think," he began, disciplining his voice to a low, even tone, "Elizabeth and Jessica Wakefield are two of the most intelligent, creative, resourceful, compassionate, and friendly girls I've ever met."

"Maybe so," the countess returned with a haughty smirk. "But as au pairs—"

"As au pairs," Laurent repeated sharply, cutting her off, "Elizabeth and Jessica are doing an excellent job. More, my brother and sisters adore them." With that he turned around, his face hot with the anger that simmered just beneath the surface.

His stepmother glanced at him just then, and obviously presuming that he and the countess were having a friendly chat, Princess Catherine gave him a broad smile of approval. Laurent sighed wearily.

The countess di Rimini gripped the back of his chair and pressed on, relentless, astonishing Laurent with her stubborn vindictiveness. "*Look* at them," she hissed into his ear. "Those girls are wearing dresses of style and worth—and they *still* manage to present an image of low-class vulgarity and cheap garishness." The countess shuddered dramatically. "That one with the darkened eyes and garish lipstick looks positively frightening."

Laurent realized she was talking about Elizabeth, and his temper snapped. *That's it*, he resolved, primed for battle. He could sense how difficult it was for Elizabeth to maintain her position on that stage, her heart bleeding after having been ripped to shreds that very morning.

By me, Laurent reminded himself. Waves of guilt and remorse crashed over him. He knew with gut certainty that he'd never forgive himself for the pain he'd caused Elizabeth. *But I'm not going to stand by and let her be insulted by this nasty, ignorant snob!*

"And her sister, the *fairy godmother,*" the countess uttered snidely.

Laurent turned around fully and glared at her. "If you dislike the tableau so strongly, then I suggest you leave!"

The countess suddenly blanched. Her jaw dropped, and her eyes blazed with a look of shocked rage. A choking gasp escaped from her open mouth.

Laurent was surprised by her reaction. He hadn't thought his words would pack such a wallop, especially on someone as dense and self-righteous as the countess. Then he realized that she wasn't even looking at him. Her eyes were fixed on something in the *Cinderella* tableau.

Elizabeth silently counted the passing seconds to distract herself as she maintained her pose in the tableau. She'd done the math in her head—there were three hundred seconds in five minutes, and she had more than two hundred seconds left to go. Then the timer would buzz, signaling the end of her torture.

Elizabeth wondered if her evil-stepmother scowl would last that long. Her lips were already twitching with cramps, and the muscles in her neck and jaw felt as if they'd turned to stone. She had an itch behind her left knee, and something sharp was poking her upper back.

Elizabeth felt totally miserable on the inside too. Despair and heartbreak hovered at the edge of her thoughts, threatening her composure. She didn't look into the audience for fear that she might catch a glimpse of Laurent.

Elizabeth knew that without the constant distraction of counting off the seconds, her mind would drift into the danger zone. She would probably fall apart and have to finish the rest of the tableau as a sobbing heap in the middle of the stage.

Elizabeth felt a glimmer of relief when she mentally counted up to two hundred and forty—the tableau would last only one more minute. The itch behind her left knee had spread to include her ankle, her elbow, and a spot just above her lips.

Suddenly Elizabeth heard the countess di Rimini's voice shriek angrily. The children reacted immediately. Manon threw her arms around Elizabeth's legs and hid her face in the stepmother costume. Claudine dropped her foot, Pierre jumped up, and both of them looked to the twins for reassurance.

Elizabeth's heart sank. All their hard work, everything she'd endured . . . it had all been for nothing.

Then she got mad. *That woman has gone too far this time,* she thought.

She and Jessica exchanged meaningful looks. Elizabeth understood that her twin felt the same way. They turned toward the audience and faced the rude heckler together.

The countess was standing close to the stage. "Shameless," she raged, glaring at the twins. Then she whirled around and stormed out of the parlor.

Later that evening Jessica stood in front of the mirror in her bedroom, inspecting her appearance. The lavender silk ball gown had been an inspired choice. It fit her perfectly, as if it had been created especially for her. The full skirt swirled gracefully when she moved. She was wearing long white gloves that covered her arms up to her elbows and gave her an especially sophisticated formal look. The gloves would have covered her new bracelet, so she'd decided to wear it with the pearls around her ankle instead.

Jessica picked up her emerald pendant and held it to her neck. She still hadn't decided whether to wear it to the ball or not. "I think it's beautiful," she declared. But Jacques's words still rang in her ears, mocking her for admiring such a "garish piece of junk."

For several minutes Jessica debated with herself, picking up the stone and putting it back down. *Since when do I let other people dictate my style!* she fumed. She was sick of royal snobs and their superior attitudes. Jacques would soon learn that she wasn't the sort of girl he could push around.

Jessica put the chain around her neck and smiled at her reflection. The pendant shimmered in the light from her lamp. "I'm wearing it tonight, and no one is going to stop me," she declared.

She rotated the clasp to the front to fasten it, then adjusted it so that the pendant draped in a graceful V at the base of her throat. The effect was absolutely stunning. Jessica exhaled a deep, satisfied sigh.

Just then she heard a heavy knock at her door. "Come in, Liz," she responded, presuming it was her twin. Jessica hoped that Elizabeth's spirits had lifted since their disastrous tableau.

But when the door burst open, the countess di Rimini marched into the room, with two armed guards behind her. The witch pointed to Jessica's pendant and shouted, "That's it! The girl is a thief!" The countess raged in English.

Jessica stepped back, stunned. "What!" she exclaimed. "How dare you accuse me!"

One of the guards came forward. "How long have you had that piece of jewelry?" he asked.

"Since my boyfriend gave it to me," she retorted.

"Enough!" the countess bellowed at the guards. "I want her locked up immediately. You can ask your questions later." Her thin lips twisted into a cruel smile. "I'm sure her answers will be much more truthful after she's spent a night in the dungeon."

"No!" Jessica pleaded. "I can explain everything. . . . I didn't steal it. . . ."

Heedless to her cries, the guards grabbed her by her arms and dragged her out of her room.

Chapter 13

"No more jumping on the bed, kids!" Elizabeth ordered, punctuating her words with a loud clap. She and the children were in her room, getting ready for the ball.

"My bow fell off again," Manon complained, holding the pink barrette up to Elizabeth.

"Come here," Elizabeth said with an indulgent smile. She brushed Manon's hair and reattached the bow-shaped barrette. "It would stay there if you'd stop jumping around like a little rabbit."

"I want to dress up like a rabbit next time when we play tableau," Manon immediately declared.

Elizabeth groaned inwardly. *Let's hope there never is a next time,* she thought, recalling the countess's rude behavior during their tableau.

The countess was a one-woman riot starter, stirring up hot tempers wherever she was. Only a few minutes earlier Elizabeth had heard her shrieking in the hall. Totally uninterested, she'd stayed in her room with her door firmly closed. She hadn't felt curious enough to find out what the commotion was about or even to peek out of her room.

Elizabeth turned her attention to her reflection in the mirror. Except for some puffiness around her eyes, she looked fine. She was wearing an elegant gown of white brocade, with a fitted bodice and thin straps over the shoulders.

Elizabeth slipped a pair of silky white gloves over her arms and looked at the effect in the mirror. "Nice!" she exclaimed.

She was surprised to see herself actually smiling. *I'm beautiful,* she thought confidently. *Those witches haven't knocked me down yet—and they never will!* she vowed.

"OK, everyone line up for a group inspection." The children rushed over and squeezed together in front of the mirror, giggling.

Earlier that evening Elizabeth had dreaded having to take charge of the children. But she owed it to Jessica, who had stayed with them at the tableau while Elizabeth had escaped to her room for a long, hard cry.

But now, laughing at their hilarious expressions as they preened in front of the mirror,

Elizabeth realized that the children had helped lighten her gloomy mood. Despite everything that had gone wrong that day, she wasn't filled with dread at the thought of walking into the ball. No matter what anyone said, deep in her heart Elizabeth knew Laurent loved her as much as she loved him. Antonia di Rimini meant nothing to him.

Elizabeth exhaled a deep sigh. Maybe she would even muster up the courage to confront him with the question that burned in her mind—why was he planning to marry a girl he didn't love. . . .

From the corner of her eye Elizabeth noticed Pierre and Claudine exchange mysterious looks. "What's going on?" she asked, glaring at them in the mirror.

"Don't tell her," Pierre insisted.

Elizabeth folded her arms. "I'm waiting. . . ."

"It's a secret," Claudine explained.

Elizabeth pulled Manon away and bent down to her level. "You'll tell me what they're up to, won't you, sweetie?"

"Maybe they want to dress up as bunny rabbits too," Manon offered.

Elizabeth rose to her full height and leaned against the door. She knew Claudine and Pierre were up to no good, and she feared they might be planning to pull a prank at the ball. Elizabeth refused to risk another public humiliation. "No one leaves this room until you tell me the secret," she announced.

Claudine's jaw dropped. "Forever?"

Elizabeth nodded. "You're my prisoners."

Finally Pierre cracked. "We found a place at the beach where there's lots of little crabs. Tomorrow we're going to go there and catch them." He lowered his voice to a whisper. "And then we're going to dump them out in the countess di Rimini's bed."

"We know where she sleeps," Claudine added.

Elizabeth pressed her hand to her mouth to keep herself from bursting out laughing.

"Here she comes!" Pierre gasped.

Elizabeth frowned, wondering what he meant. Then she heard it too: heavy footsteps and the countess's loud voice bellowing out commands and threats. Elizabeth slouched back against her door and crossed her arms. *Doesn't that nasty hag ever take a rest?* she thought.

The commotion grew louder and louder. Suddenly Elizabeth's door was thrown open, knocking her to the floor with its force. She landed heavily on her side, her elbow slamming against the hardwood floor. Elizabeth groaned at the sharp, pinching pain that shot up and down her arm.

Elizabeth lifted her head and turned around, her eyes wide with shock and anger.

The countess was standing over her, snarling like a vicious, rabid dog. Elizabeth almost expected to see foamy saliva spewing all over the woman's fleshy jowls. She was accompanied by two uniformed guards, who came forward and roughly hauled Elizabeth up by her arms.

"What is going on?" Elizabeth demanded as she struggled to loosen her arms out of the guards' tight hold.

The children looked terrified as they huddled together on the small, four-poster bed, sobbing hysterically. The countess approached them. Manon buried her face in the pillow.

"Go away!" Pierre screamed.

Tears pooled in Elizabeth's eyes, blurring her vision. The sound of the children's frightened cries pierced her heart like hot daggers. "Leave the kids alone!" she pleaded.

The witch whirled around, her eyes blazing. "You have no right to hand out orders, young lady."

Elizabeth flinched, as if she'd been slapped across the face. *Why does this person hate me so much?* she wondered.

The countess stepped closer to the children. "Don't be afraid," she cooed in French in a shrill, evil-sounding voice. "Your au pair girls are very bad criminals—they've stolen something very valuable from me. But we're going to lock them up so they can't hurt you."

"What?" Elizabeth gasped, enraged. "That's a lie! We haven't stolen anything from you, and you know it!"

The countess jerked her head around and waved dismissal with her arm. "Take her out of my sight," she commanded the guards. "Her face sickens me."

Elizabeth struggled desperately to get free as the guards dragged her toward the door. The children screamed and begged them not to take her away.

"Go to Anna," Elizabeth shouted to them. "And don't be afraid. This is all a big mistake. I'll be fine, and I'll probably see you later at the ball."

But as the guards led her to the back of the château and down a cold stone staircase, Elizabeth hoped her parting words to the children hadn't been a lie.

Alone in his cottage, Laurent gazed at the fire burning in the hearth. He was scheduled to make his entrance at the ball in twenty minutes. Guests from all over the world had been arriving at the château since the previous evening.

After this evening my days of freedom are over for good, Laurent realized with a sinking feeling in his gut. He braced his elbows on his knees and hung his head. His future seemed to spread out before him like a barren, desolate trail. *If only I had the girl I love at my side . . . ,* he thought. He pictured himself and Elizabeth standing together at the ball as everyone cheered their announcement and wished them well. . . .

Laurent squeezed his eyes shut in a feeble attempt to block the image from his mind. It hurt to think about what might have been. But Elizabeth's beautiful face continued to haunt him, as he knew it would for the rest of his life.

Laurent rubbed his hand over his mouth and sat back, staring at the ceiling. The burden of his duty and honor weighed him down like a huge marble slab strapped to his back. And now he'd dragged Elizabeth down too.

A knock at the door caught him by surprise. His heart leaped to his throat. Lately the only person who ever dropped by unexpectedly had been Elizabeth. *Please let it be her,* he hoped as he rushed across the room. He longed to hold her one last time . . . and kiss her sweet lips . . . and hear her say that she loved him. . . .

Laurent's hands trembled as he unlatched the door. But it was his father who stood there. Laurent's heart plummeted with bitter disappointment.

Prince Nicolas walked into the cottage with a purposeful stride, his face drawn into a grim expression. "I have something to tell you." He spoke in French, his voice low and serious. "Sit down, Laurent. This might be difficult for you to hear."

Antonia has broken our engagement? Laurent thought snidely as he returned to the couch.

"The American girls have betrayed our trust," his father told him.

Laurent stiffened. "What do you mean?" he demanded.

Prince Nicolas sat down in the chair across from Laurent and leaned forward. "They've been implicated in the theft of the countess di Rimini's emerald."

"That's ridiculous!" Laurent retorted. "That woman has been out to destroy Elizabeth and Jessica from the moment they arrived. You saw her at the tableau! She was rude and disruptive."

His father shook his head gravely. "That doesn't change the facts, son. Those girls are thieves—and liars. I shudder to think of how we trusted them with the little ones."

"It's simply not true," Laurent argued. "Whatever the countess may have said—"

"The guards found the countess's pendant less than an hour ago," Prince Nicolas told him. "And do you know where?"

Laurent rubbed his knuckle against his lips as he stared at his father. "Where?" he challenged.

"In their quarters," his father replied. "Hanging from a gold chain around one of their necks."

Laurent reeled back, as if he had been socked in the jaw. "I still don't believe it. Elizabeth and Jessica are not thieves!"

His father gave him a sympathetic look. "I know you trusted them. We all did," he admitted. "There's a lesson to be learned from our mistake. The only ones you can trust in this world are people like yourself, people on equal footing who have no need or desire to steal from you."

Laurent's temper flared. "That's ridiculous, Father! It's that kind of nonsense that keeps us locked in the Middle Ages."

Prince Nicolas exhaled wearily. "You can't argue with the evidence. Those girls were caught with the stolen emerald. Isn't that enough to convince you of their guilt?" he questioned. "Or would you prefer to hold your judgment until one of them shows up wearing the di Riminis' diamond necklace?"

"No!" Laurent shouted. But deep in his mind a kernel of doubt existed. "Elizabeth and her sister can't be guilty," he insisted.

"Are you trying to convince me of their innocence?" his father asked pointedly. "Or yourself?"

Laurent clenched his jaw. His father's barb had struck a nerve. "I already know they're innocent," he stated. But even to his ears, his voice sounded slightly weaker.

Elizabeth . . . a thief? Laurent wondered, forcing himself to consider the difficult possibility. He had fallen for her so quickly and completely. Maybe he *was* blinded by his strong feelings. He closed his eyes and groaned to himself. Maybe it was safer to stick to tradition and duty and to forget about love. . . .

Prince Nicolas rose to his feet. "I must return to the château now," he commented, adding, "you're expected to arrive on time this evening." He offered his hand to Laurent.

Laurent hesitated. Finally, with a deep sigh, he stood up and shook hands with his father. "I'll be there," he promised as he walked him to the door.

"Never oppose the countess unless you absolutely must," Prince Nicolas warned. "She's an important ally. Likewise, she would prove to be a formidable foe."

Laurent nodded. He knew his father was right. The countess di Rimini wielded power in both social and political circles. But the thought of having her as a mother-in-law turned his stomach.

Curled up in a fetal position on the hard stone floor, Jessica sobbed. The sound echoed in the cavernous dungeon, as if the walls were mocking her cries. She thought of Jacques and her life back in Sweet Valley. "What if I never get out of here?" she wailed. No one who might be able to help her knew where she was. *I don't even know where I am,* she realized.

Her one last hope was Elizabeth. As twins they shared a deep connection and often sensed when the other was in trouble. *Please find me, Elizabeth!* Jessica's mind screamed desperately. *I need you!*

She heard someone coming and jumped to her feet. Standing on tiptoes, she peered through the small barred window in the heavy wooden door. Two burly guards were dragging her sister toward the cell. Jessica's heart sank.

The guards swung open the door of her cell with a loud, metal clang. They thrust Elizabeth to the floor.

"She says to leave them secured," one of the guards reminded the other.

Jessica knew exactly who "she" referred to. *I'd like to choke the living daylights out of that countess*, she fumed. The guards chained Elizabeth and Jessica to the wall with metal cuffs around their wrists and ankles.

"Please don't do this," Elizabeth begged, tears streaming down her face. "You don't understand!"

The guards ignored her. With a heavy clang, they slammed the huge wood and metal door on the twins.

"I don't understand any of this!" Jessica cried. "That pendant they accused me of stealing isn't even valuable." She rubbed her back against the rough surface of the stone wall to scratch an itch. At this point it hardly mattered if she ruined the silk gown.

"You're sure?" Elizabeth asked tearfully.

Jessica nodded. "Jacques told me the stone was fake when he gave it to me on the train. He gave me the pearl bracelet to replace the emerald." She glanced at her ankle and let out an angry groan of disappointment. "It's gone. It must have fallen off when those goons dragged me down here."

Elizabeth smoothed her white gown over her knees. Jessica saw that it was stained and ripped along the hem. "You would have looked beautiful at the ball," Jessica murmured.

"Thanks," Elizabeth replied glumly. "I'll bet this doesn't have anything to do with the jewelry. The countess has it in for me because of my relationship with Laurent. I'm convinced she would stop at nothing to get me out of the way—even if it means framing us for jewel theft and locking us up in this dungeon."

Dragging her chains on the floor, Jessica reached over and patted Elizabeth's hand. "Don't worry. Jacques knows this castle inside out. He'll save us."

Elizabeth sighed wearily. "Laurent does too. The question is—do they know we're down here?"

"Jacques will find us. I'm sure of it," Jessica said. But inside, she wasn't so sure. She'd left him with some very harsh words. *What if he thinks I really don't want to see him anymore and goes away for good?* she worried. A feeling of cold panic moved through Jessica's body, like ice water in her veins. *What if no one ever finds us?*

Elizabeth turned to her with a blank expression. "There's something I don't understand," she said. "If Jacques gave you the bracelet to *replace* the pendant, why did you still have the pendant?"

Jessica cracked a tiny smile. "He wanted me to get rid of it. He claimed it was too junky for me," she explained. "But I refused to go along with him. He even tried to sneak it out of my room a few times." Tears sprang into her eyes as she recalled their many scrimmages over the emerald. "We had so much fun fighting over that emerald," she added wistfully.

Elizabeth narrowed her eyes and shook her head. "Jessica, that doesn't make sense. Why would he have bothered with the emerald if it were a fake?"

Jessica chewed her bottom lip as a disturbing possibility began to take shape in her mind. *Jacques was on the train when the countess screamed about her stolen heirloom,* she remembered. He had given it to her just before he'd gotten off the train.

She thought back to the times she'd spent with Jacques at the château. He'd always made excuses to go to her room, and she'd caught him red-handed several times. Jessica had assumed their heated scrimmages over the pendant had all been a game, a kind of flirting. *Maybe I was wrong. Maybe that emerald was the real—and only—reason for his visits to the Château D'Amour Inconnu.*

Jessica squeezed her eyes shut as pieces of a frightening puzzle fell into place. *Jacques is the thief,* she realized. *He's the one who framed me!*

She didn't want to believe any of it, but the truth was like a wailing scream tearing through her mind, shattering her heart like glass. *Elizabeth and I might be left in this medieval dungeon to die . . . because of Jacques Landeau!*

Well, it looks like both Elizabeth's and Jessica's romances have fizzled. And now they've been thrown into the dungeon, with seemingly no hope of escape! Will Jacques and Laurent redeem themselves and come to the twins' rescue? Find out in Sweet Valley High 134, **Happily Ever After,** *the third book in an enchanting three-part miniseries—coming soon. It's a fairy tale come true!*

Bantam Books in the Sweet Valley High series
Ask your bookseller for the books you have missed

SIGN UP FOR THE SWEET VALLEY HIGH® FAN CLUB!

Hey, girls! Get all the gossip on Sweet Valley High's® most popular teenagers when you join our fantastic Fan Club! As a member, you'll get all of this really cool stuff:

- Membership Card with your own personal Fan Club ID number
- A Sweet Valley High® Secret Treasure Box
- Sweet Valley High® Stationery
- Official Fan Club Pencil (for secret note writing!)
- Three Bookmarks
- A "Members Only" Door Hanger
- Two Skeins of J. & P. Coats® Embroidery Floss with flower barrette instruction leaflet
- Two editions of *The Oracle* newsletter
- Plus exclusive Sweet Valley High® product offers, special savings, contests, and much more!

Be the first to find out what Jessica & Elizabeth Wakefield are up to by joining the Sweet Valley High® Fan Club for the one-year membership fee of only $6.25 each for U.S. residents, $8.25 for Canadian residents (U.S. currency). Includes shipping & handling.

Send a check or money order (do not send cash) made payable to "Sweet Valley High® Fan Club" along with this form to:

SWEET VALLEY HIGH® FAN CLUB, BOX 3919-B, SCHAUMBURG, IL 60168-3919

NAME_____
(Please print clearly)

ADDRESS_____

CITY_____ STATE _____ ZIP_____
(Required)

AGE_____ BIRTHDAY_____ /_____ /_____

Offer good while supplies last. Allow 6-8 weeks after check clearance for delivery. Addresses without ZIP codes cannot be honored. Offer good in USA & Canada only. Void where prohibited by law.
©1993 by Francine Pascal   LCI-1383-193